I0746366

ABOUT THE AUTHOR

When Chris Behrsin isn't out exploring the world, he's behind a keyboard writing tales of dragons and magical lands. Born into the genre through a steady diet of Terry Pratchett, his fiction fuses a love for fantasy and whimsical plots with philosophy and voyages into the worlds of dreams.

You can learn more about his fiction and download two free books at his website, chrisbehrsin.com.

facebook.com/chrisbehrsin

twitter.com/chrisbehrsin

goodreads.com/cbehrsin

bookbub.com/authors/chris-behrsin

BOOKS BY CHRIS BEHRSIN

DRAGONCAT SERIES

A Cat's Guide to Bonding with Dragons

A Cat's Guide to Meddling with Magic

A Cat's Guide to Saving the Kingdom

A Cat's Guide to Questing for Treasure

A Cat's Guide to Travelling through Portals

A Cat's Guide to Vanquishing Evil

A Cat's Guide to Dreaming of Fairies

A Cat's Guide to Serving a Warlock (Prequel Novella)

SECICAO BLIGHT SERIES

Sukina's Story (Prequel Novel)

Dragonseer

Dragonseers and Bloodlines

Dragonseers and Automatons

Dragonseers and Evolution

More works available at: https://chrisbehrsin.com

A CAT'S GUIDE TO DREAMING OF FAIRIES

CHRIS BEHRSIN

A Cat's Guide to Dreaming of Fairies Copyright © 2023 by Chris Behrsin.

All Rights Reserved.

No part of this book may be reproduced in any form or by any electronic or mechanical means including information storage and retrieval systems, without permission in writing from the author. The only exception is by a reviewer, who may quote short excerpts in a review.

This book is a work of fiction. Names, characters, places, and incidents either are products of the author's imagination or are used fictitiously. Any resemblance to actual persons, living or dead, events, or locales is entirely coincidental.

Copyediting by Tarryn Thomas (https://tarrynthomas.com)
Cover Design Layout by Chris Behrsin

ISBN: 978-1-915886-48-4 (paperback)
ISBN: 978-1-915886-47-7 (hardcover)
ISBN: 978-1-915886-46-0 (e-book)

Published by Worldwalkers Publishing Ltd

For Raffles

THE STORY SO FAR ...

You probably already know who I am, but for posterity's sake I'll state it outright.

My name is Ben in the human language, and I'm a Bengal, descendant of the great Asian leopard cat and the mighty George, vanquisher of warlocks, and recent acolyte of the mighty goddess of cats, Bastet herself. My story, by the time you're reading this, will have already spread across the dimensions.

Yet there's so much story that still needs to be told.

It all started when I was yanked across time and space – from my comfortable breakfast of salmon trimmings in South Wales onto the cold stone floor of the evil grey-eyed warlock Astravar – to do his bidding in another dimension. He wanted me for the purpose of catching demon rats.

But I wasn't having any of that ...

I was soon out of the door, bonding with my ruby dragon Salanraja, then gaining magic and the gift of speaking all languages, crossing multiple dimensions through magical portals, and eventually gaining the ability to defeat Astravar. I didn't do that without a little help from my dragon rider friends, of course, not to mention the former Fae turned Cat Sidhe Ta'ra.

We also had the help of our magical crystals; these exist across the dimensions and are the source of my magic and all my other abilities. Without them, I doubt I would have come so far.

Of course, that is never the end of it, and a new warlock entered the fray just as Astravar had left it. Our new nemesis was the wicked Warlock Prince, Arran, once the king's nephew until the king denounced him.

Thus even more upheaval ensued, as Arran involved the King of Chaos in the Seventh Dimension, the mighty demon snake Apopis, and gained access to *Cana Dei* – the dark force that expands across dimensions and has the sole purpose of turning every living thing into a lifeless drone.

Cana Dei eventually took over Arran's soul, and using him as its puppet again, almost destroyed every one of the dimensions except the void itself. But unfortunately for its vile plans, I had new allies on the scene – a brilliant and beautiful alabaster Abyssinian called Esme, who was also a daughter of Bastet, and not to forget the dog who, after swallowing a magical key, could flick between dimensions as if they were television channels without the use of portals. He's also a Sussex spaniel by the way, and his name is Max.

Oh, and we enlisted the aid of Bastet herself, but let me not get ahead of myself.

Now under the thrall of Cana Dei, Arran decided he would target the Fifth Dimension with a nefarious plan. There, Bastet guards all the souls of every single living creature across all the dimensions – pink glowing things within glass containers that rest at the edge of a dark river. *Cana Dei*, if it reached those souls, could have destroyed them in an instant. We would have become lifeless servants of that dark force, without any living purpose. I couldn't think of a fate worse than that.

But it wasn't going to happen if we could stop it ...

Arran almost killed Bastet, and then there was a massive battle, humans, dragons, and unicorns pitted against demons and *Cana Dei*. We won, of course, and it wasn't me but Max who knocked Arran into the Eighth Dimension – the void from which there is no return.

I did my part, of course, and a mighty one it was too. I knocked Arran's demon hellhound into the abyss. I didn't do it in cat form, though, but as a chimera – the crystals having gifted me with the ability to turn into one. Not permanently, thank the whiskers; I don't want to lose my beautiful Bengal form, thank you very much.

After all that, you would have thought we'd have had a chance to rest.

But alas, you can never close all the doors in the world; some will always be left open.

The demons still inhabited the Seventh Dimension. Apopis might have been greatly weakened, but it seemed the crocodile-hippopotamus Ammit still wanted revenge. Six evil warlocks also remained in the First Dimension, and we all wondered when they would eventually strike. During our more recent adventures, we had invertedly allowed Lasinta to touch the Grand Crystal in the looming Tower of the Grand inside shining Cimlean City, though we had no idea what the consequences would be.

I also still had my friend, Ta'ra, to worry about. She had gone back to re-join her former fairy husband in the verdant and vivid Faerie Realm, aka the Second Dimension. There the air always smells rich with pollen, and the rivers dance, and the waterfalls roar, and the shining golden wisps fly here and there. They say that the Faerie Realm is the most beautiful of them all, and I guess I felt a little jealous that Ta'ra got to live there.

She was born into that life, though. Before I'd met her, and Astravar had cast the spell to turn her into a Cait Sidhe, Ta'ra had been betrothed to the fairy prince Ta'lon. She was meant to become a fairy princess.

Problem was, Ta'ra was no longer fairy, but a cat. Astravar's antics had permanently changed her into one. But she'd disappointed me when she'd said that she still wanted to be a fairy and live with her former kin. Her former betrothed and his court thought that they could hide her form behind a glamour spell and pretend that she was still a fairy.

Oh, how wrong they were.

Honestly, I'd thought Ta'ra was gone for good ... I'd thought I'd lost her forever.

I was wrong of course. Because I had no idea how her feline existence would influence the events that were about to unfold. I dreamt of her the night just before the new school year.

That was the night that the chaos started, and it is on that night that my story continues ...

BEAUTIFUL DREAMS

The black cat stalked across the Faerie Realm, her slender body swaying with each narrow and careful step. Ta'ra hadn't always walked so elegantly – she had been a clumsy cat when I'd first met her.

But then I had trained her how to carry herself with grace, and she had been a good student. Now as I watched her in my dream she seemed the most beautiful cat of them all.

More beautiful than Esme ... The thought came to me at that single moment, and I felt immediately guilty for thinking it. After all, I was curled up in the real world with my back pressed against the soft warmth of Esme's chest. I could feel her breathing there, with deep confident breaths.

Esme – one of Bastet's daughters, an Abyssinian with rich shiny white fur and a pink nose perfectly placed at the tip of her tapered face. She was my *companion* now, the cat that I thought I'd spend the rest of my long life with.

But toms like me aren't meant to have a single *companion*, and Esme had none of the allure that Ta'ra had right now in my dream, in this luxuriant, vivid Faerie Realm.

Wisps of shiny pollen drifted down from the cherry blossoms high up in the pink trees that surrounded Ta'ra. The Faerie Realm – also called the Second Dimension – is the only place I know where you can actually see pollen. It floats on the air like faint wisps of steam, occasionally catching the sunlight. Everything here is so incredibly textured, and the whole place is much more colourful than anywhere I've never known. There is no room for bleakness in the Faerie Realm.

All around me the air smelled of different kinds of flowers, and had the latent warmth and humidity that never seems to leave the place. I could literally taste the honey that the bees, darting from petal to petal, would produce from the pollen they were taking to their hives.

Ta'ra looked over her shoulder, and I wondered if for a moment she knew I was there. With her richly alluring green eyes, she blinked twice, slowly and surely.

I didn't have a body here yet, but I didn't need one. I didn't need eyes, or a nose, or a mouth, or any other organ with which to sense this world. After all, this was a dream and so normal rules didn't apply.

Ta'ra turned away and stalked onwards. I floated after her, completely mesmerised by the dance of her body as she wove her way through the long grass.

Not a fairy – a cat. Always a cat. She couldn't hide it anymore.

But what would the fairies think if they saw her displaying her true, natural form?

The stalks of grass parted, and dragonflies danced away as Ta'ra dashed through the meadow. I swayed after her, floating just slightly behind and above her tail, as if I were attached to the tip of it and being pulled along.

She emerged into a wide glade boasting a crystal-clear lake, which reflected the lush, distant, rolling hills. Clearly she wasn't here for the lake, as she almost immediately turned her head to watch a rat that had its nose to the mulchy ground, tracking something. It didn't know that Ta'ra was there, and I could almost feel the vibrations in Ta'ra's paws as she tracked its every movement, not taking her eyes off the target.

She lowered herself onto her haunches, and now as I hovered in front of her I noticed her whiskers twitching slightly before she pounced. She darted right through me, and then beyond onto the rat, her prey. So elegantly done ... Just as I'd taught her, but somehow better.

I'd trained Ta'ra for this, but now from the way she moved I felt she could teach me many things. The student had become the master, and I respected her so much more.

But was this actually real? It was a dream, surely. What was I doing here in the Faerie Realm?

Ta'ra backed away from the rat, and I hovered over it to see it smoking. It wasn't a normal rodent; if you looked closely enough, you could see the cracks in its craggy skin and smell the brimstone burning within it. A demon rat from the Seventh Dimension – what was it doing here in the Faerie Realm?

I danced to one side, and Ta'ra looked over towards me again. The dark wells in her bright green eyes had filled with power. They didn't look normal anymore. I knew that look – she was possessed.

A bright light flashed in front of me. A portal, tearing the sky apart, leading out into a dark world. Only a fairy in the Second Dimension could open a portal to another realm. The fairies protected the land that way.

Did Ta'ra count as a fairy in this respect? Could she still open portals? In all honesty, I didn't know.

An elderly woman stepped out of the portal. In fact, elderly was an understatement. She looked so old, the wrinkles so unnaturally deep, her eyes so sunken into her cavernous face, that every bend in her posture made it seem as if she were defying death.

I knew her.

Lasinta – the leader of the warlocks and their chief – our mortal enemy and now the most feared magic user in all the realms. In the first dimension, no one had heard from her for months.

I began to smell the horrid stench of dark magic, which was just like rotten vegetable juice. I hate that smell – it doesn't belong in any world.

The old woman stopped just outside the portal, then clicked her dry fingers to close it. A dark crystal, grey and lifeless, fell from her hand and tinkled when it hit the ground. Lasinta brushed the dust off her purple cloak and then her gaze roved downwards.

Ta'ra was frozen to the spot. Her only signs of life were the way her tail swished very slowly and the shallow rise and fall of her chest. She stared up at the ancient warlock as if in supplication.

When Lasinta saw Ta'ra looking at her in this way, her thin mouth curled upwards. I don't think I could describe it as a smile – the expression was far too wicked for that. Lasinta turned her head to the side and then her gaze fell on the demon rat lying there dead on the floor. She bent down and picked it up, then turned it around in her hands to examine it.

"Thank you once again, dear fairy," she said. "You shall have your wish, and I shall have mine."

Her eyes crinkled as she lifted a staff off her back. It was made of smooth dark wood, and at the top of it a purple crystal shone dimly. Purple mist rose from the verdant ground; it enshrouded the grass stalks and they curled into blackness. From everywhere came the stench of rotten vegetable juice, and I knew what we were looking at now – the darkest of all possible magic, filled only with evil intent.

In the real world, my breath must have caught in my throat, because I found myself coughing. I watched in terror as Lasinta pointed her staff at Ta'ra. From it shot forth a purple beam, and I wanted to scream out, "No!"

But the word wouldn't come. After all, I had no substance in this world; no fairy had let me in through a portal. I wasn't meant to be here.

The beam hit Ta'ra square on the white diamond marking on her chest. A glow expanded outwards at the impact point. In Ta'ra's eyes I saw the wicked reflection of it, and her pupils dilated even more.

I heard something buzz nearby. Swiftly beating wings let out a high-pitched sound, and a golden glow floated over. A plume of golden smoke mingled with the purple mist that continued to rise up out of the ground.

From inside of the golden plume arose a man with dark oily hair, hard cheekbones, and an unnaturally white toothy smile. He wore a lime green velvet shirt and a yellow cloak embroidered with bees and butterflies. One day this fairy would be crowned king of the entire realm.

Prince Ta'lon – Ta'ra's betrothed – working with Lasinta.

But this was just a dream, wasn't it? This couldn't be real … I didn't like Ta'lon, but he wouldn't betray us in this way, would he? Surely not …

Lasinta continued to work her magic on Ta'ra. Her cat form – Ta'ra's beautiful cat form – faded. Then, out of the blend of golden and purple gases, there emerged a human woman. She was smaller than most humans I knew, and slight of stature, with raven hair and a black cloak. A white frilly blouse poked out of the neck of her cape.

I'd only seen Ta'ra's human glamour a couple of times, and I much, much preferred her as a cat.

Ta'ra's pupils were still wide open, welling even deeper within her dark brown irises. She seemed lost, not knowing anything that was happening around her. But then, once she had become fully human, and once Lasinta had cut off her magic, a moment of recognition seemed to dawn on Ta'ra and her pupils constricted rapidly, looking just as they should in such bright light.

She sniffed the air, as if she were still a cat, then turned her head and looked straight at me – or at least at the point where I floated, bodiless. "Help me, Ben ... I'm trapp—"

"Silence!" Lasinta cried, cutting her off. Another purple beam shot out of her staff and hit her right between the eyes. Ta'ra's pupils quickly expanded again, and she exhaled, letting out a deep sigh.

Lasinta turned her head towards me, and in the real world I felt my body shudder. She frowned. "Hmm ..."

"I have your payment, warlock," Ta'lon said.

Lasinta shook her head and turned her attention back to him. He carried a beige leather pouch in his right hand.

Lasinta took the pouch from him and weighed it in her palm. "An ounce of it," she said. "No less, though I wouldn't complain if you supplied more."

"To the weight of a feather."

"And I trust you're already processing the next week's supply, because we will not tolerate any more delays."

Ta'lon looked over at Ta'ra. She turned her head towards him, and a smile appeared between her thin lips. But I didn't need to be a human to tell that it was fake.

"There will be no more delays," Ta'lon said. "I've already punished those responsible."

"Good," Lasinta said. "Then enjoy your month of *matrimony*. She looks much better in this form, to my mind. I don't know what Astravar was thinking."

She turned slightly. I heard some leaves rustling, and Ta'lon shuffled on the spot. "Of course," he said, "we'll be able to quadruple your payment if you can make this change permanent. The whole family ... we want the princess back for good."

Lasinta paused, and she studied Ta'lon over her shoulder. "Maybe I will, one day ... but first we need to establish a relationship of trust between the warlocks and the fairies. Do you think that such an allegiance is possible?"

Ta'lon tugged at the collar of his velvet shirt. "These things are always possible, given the right conditions."

The corners of Lasinta's eyes curled upwards. "Then we shall have to see what transpires."

She didn't say another word, and I guessed no more needed to be said. Rather, the old lady turned on her heel and stepped out of the portal, back onto the barren earth of the Wastelands.

As the white glowing halo of the portal shrunk to close her out, she turned to look over her shoulder again. Her gaze seemed to fall right on me, and it was as if she knew I was there.

I turned back, but I no longer saw Ta'lon and Ta'ra standing there, but instead two golden wisps dancing away amidst the shining pollen on the breeze.

I wanted to stay here; I wanted to do anything I could to protect Ta'ra, to help her in any way I could. But this was a dream after all, and in the real world my tummy was rumbling.

I didn't need a portal to lift me out of the Faerie Realm. All I needed was for someone to shout the magic words ...

"Breakfast is ready!"

2

LEAVE MY MACKEREL ALONE

The smell of smoked mackerel wafting over to my nostrils made me forget all about being in the Faerie Realm – at least for the moment. I opened my eyes to see three bowls laid out before me on the stone floor of Aleam's workshop.

This was Dragonsbond Academy – the castle in which it had taken me so long to realise that I belonged. After our sojourn at the School of the White in Cimlean City, Bastet had taught us how to handle white magic, knighting us as her Guardians of the White, and so we had no need to study alongside the smelly unicorns anymore.

Thus I was now living with another cat and a dog in Aleam's workshop in this castle. Soon a new year would start, and we'd be back to studying how to become full-fledged dragon riders. A couple more years and I would be protecting the kingdom from warlocks with a staff in my mouth, riding on a dragon's back.

That was if the warlocks ever decided to attack; we'd not had dealings with them now for around a month.

Esme was slowly sampling the mackerel in the first bowl,

savouring every mouthful and chewing slowly, as if she had all the time in the world to eat it. In the centre, Max the smelly Sussex spaniel, who had once had the ability to walk between the dimensions, wolfed down his food in large bites, and he'd almost emptied the second bowl. If I didn't hurry, he'd start on my breakfast too, and then there'd be no smoked mackerel for poor old Ben.

I leaped off the feather cushion on the bench underneath the open window. Behind me I could hear the sparrows chittering outside; these were the sounds of early autumn and the start of a new school year. Sunlight streamed through the window, and motes of dust danced in my path on the way to my bowl.

Max was nearly finished his food. His shaggy fur trailed all the way down to the ground; it had also grown over the ankh symbol that decorated the side of his chest – the brand he'd acquired when he'd gained the ability to walk between the dimensions. He could no longer do so, but still the fur was slightly greyer there.

He turned his head towards my bowl, sniffing with his big wet nose on the end of his long snout. He had his droopy ears folded right down against his head. It was as if he didn't realise an extra bowl was next to him, but his sense of smell would discover it soon.

Before his gaze could fall fully on my bowl I swiped a paw across his face and batted him away from my bowl. I didn't use my claws – Max was a friend now, or at least as close to one as a dog can ever be to a cat. But still, there was no way I was letting him near my breakfast.

"Don't you dare, Max," I said. "You've had your fill, and you can always ask Aleam for more."

I spoke in the dog language, because I have the special ability to speak all languages, which was granted to me by the magical crystals. Esme could speak it too, although I'd never quite understood how.

Max whimpered, then he rubbed where I'd hit him with his front paw. It wasn't as if I'd hit him hard, but still the big softy had to whine about it.

"But I thought you didn't want breakfast," Max said.

"And what gave you that idea?"

"I thought you wanted to sleep longer. You didn't even wake when Aleam clanked the fork against the bowl."

I growled from the base of my stomach. Speaking dog, my subsequent protest came out in short sharp barks. "When will you ever learn, Max? Cats like to preserve their food. If we don't eat it immediately, then we intend to save it until later."

"But why not just eat it all at once? It's not as if the humans won't provide more food."

"That's just how it is – why do you have to ask so many questions?"

"Fine," Max said, and he turned and went to sulk in a corner.

I tried to ignore the sound of his tail thumping irritably against the floor as I lowered my nose into the third bowl. The smell of smoked mackerel washed over me, and for that single moment I was in cat heaven.

I practically inhaled a few mouthfuls of the stuff, not realising how hungry I was. Fully satisfied, I lifted my head and turned to see Esme's bright blue eyes watching me from behind her pink nose. She spoke to me in the cat language.

"You know, you did sleep pretty deeply, and you were mumbling in your dreams."

I twitched my whiskers. "Was I?"

"'Ta'ra,' you said. You were dreaming of her, Ben, weren't you?"

"I—" I stopped myself. I'd had enough dealings with

warlocks over the recent years, and I didn't want anything more to do with them.

Esme brushed her cheek gently against mine. "It's nothing to be ashamed of, Ben. We all have our histories, and I know that she is long gone for now. Just as long as we move on, right? You have me now."

I did have Esme, a daughter of Bastet and the most graceful cat I'd ever known. Her rich white fur shone brightly in the sunlight streaming through the window.

I must admit, tomcats aren't meant for only one *companion*, but having spent so much time with humans I'd started behaving just like them. Esme and I had fallen out for a while, but after our battle in the Fifth Dimension to save the realm of souls from Arran and the demons, we'd grown closer again.

Humans have this thing called love, and I wouldn't quite describe what Esme and I had as that. In all honesty I'd never understood that concept. Still, I was closer to her than to any other creature in this realm, save perhaps my dragon. But my bond with Salanraja was a very different kind of connection.

"It's good spending time with you, Esme, yes."

She chortled – a cat's chuckle, not a human one. To human ears, I guess it sounded like a soft chirp.

"While we have peace, you had better enjoy it," she said. "Because the warlocks will attack again eventually."

I wondered then if I should tell her about my dream, but then I decided that I had no need to. Dreams after all aren't real. What I'd seen was just what I wanted to believe – or at least a deep, twisted part of me did.

I'd often had fantasies that involved Ta'ra being unhappy in the Faerie Realm, and where she needed to be saved and brought back to this dimension. I would fly Salanraja in there, and I'd use both white and dark magic to battle her oppressors and fly her back into this life again. She wasn't meant to be a fairy; she was meant to be a cat.

But that probably wasn't the situation at all. She was likely in Faerini right now, eating sweet grapes and vegetables – in human form even if her cat stomach couldn't digest them, with the kind of expression that humans and fairies found pretty. She would smell of the most flowery perfume, and she would be gazing longingly into Ta'lon's eyes.

Whiskers, she'd probably even be married to him by now. She'd certainly never invited me to her wedding. But I was a cat, so why did I even care?

"Ben," Esme said. Her eyes had narrowed, and she didn't look happy with me. "Are you okay, Ben?"

"I'm just … it's nothing," I said, and I turned my nose back towards the food.

I didn't get to savour the mackerel for very long, though, before I heard another voice in my head, this time deep and female and speaking the language of the mind.

"Bengie," Salanraja – my dragon – said.

"Ben," I said. *"Why don't you ever learn that I don't like that particular nickname?"*

"Whatever," she said. *"It's not important."*

"It is important, it's my name!"

"Not now, it isn't … because that dream I saw you having … that one with Ta'ra …"

"You saw that?" I asked.

"Of course I did," Salanraja said. *"We're bonded … but now I'm watching it all over again."*

"What are you talking about, Salanraja?"

"Our crystal, Bengie. You need to come here at once."

3

DREAMS AND VISIONS

A soft blue light filled Salanraja's chamber, coming from our crystal that was propped up against the wall. Images flickered across its vast facets – familiar pictures of the colourful Faerie Realm, and of Faerini City bedecked with trees and waterfalls, and of golden fairies dancing here, there and everywhere.

This was our crystal, which we had to protect, because if it ever was destroyed we would perish with it. Crystals can exist across the dimensions and this grand faceted thing was the source of both our magic and the bond between Salanraja and me. Without crystals, no one could use magic at all – not light, dark, fairy or dragon magic.

Whiskers, without them I don't think dragons would even be able to use their fire. They'd just exist as gigantic lizards with wings, and they certainly wouldn't attach themselves to humans, or cats, or dogs, or whatever other creatures they might choose to bond with in the future.

A large opening to the outer world spanned the space behind the crystal. Outside of it extended the luxuriant fields of Dragonsbond Academy – a rich mosaic of yellow and green. The sky was clear, and so I could see the thin line of the Willowed Woods in the distance, now yellowing as autumn approached.

Salanraja stood to one side of the opening, a tall ruby-red dragon with bright yellow eyes and teeth like the fangs of a sabre tooth tiger. Two columns of spikes ran the length of her back, positioned in such a way that they formed a neat corridor that could safely contain me while she was flying. She couldn't wear a saddle because of those spikes, which was the reason that she'd ended up bonding with a cat – or so the story went.

She had a leg of dragon-flamed beef in front of her, and the smell was so tantalising that I wanted to have breakfast all over again.

"Stop it, Bengie," Salanraja said in my mind as she saw me approaching and sniffing the food. *"You're on a diet, remember?"*

I ignored the fact that she'd used my nickname again. She was just trying to annoy me, and I wasn't going to grant her the satisfaction of succeeding.

"I'm not on a diet," I replied instead.

Talk about ridiculous. This Bengal is in very good shape thank you very much.

"Didn't you say that you wanted to eat less?" Salanraja asked.

"No, I said that I wanted to stop thinking about food all the time, so I could focus my mind on loftier goals."

"Exactly – so, a diet."

"It's not a diet; I don't need to lose weight. I can eat the same amount of food, I just don't want it to control my life anymore. And you're not making it easy by having this beef laid out in front of me, letting off all its delicious smells."

"So very cat-like," Salanraja teased. *"What would Esme say?"*

"Esme ... my companion ..."

"Except now you have Ta'ra back on your mind," Salanraja said.

"Just ... stop it! What did you bring me up here to look at?"

"See for yourself ..."

Salanraja turned her head towards the crystal that had now increased in brightness as if it wanted to draw our attention. On it, I could see the dark Cat Sidhe form of Ta'ra stalking through the long grass of the Second Dimension. There was sound as well – just like you'd have on the television. I could hear the buzzing of the bees, and the distantly rushing waterfalls, and the chirping of so many different birds that I didn't think I could name them all through their calls alone.

It was just like it had been in my dream, and though I was no longer inside of it, I could still picture myself floating over Ta'ra, just as the viewpoint of the crystal was doing now. She swayed, and the scene swayed with her. Her movement – it was hypnotic, though I also had a tight fear in my gut of what was coming next.

"Is this the past," I asked Salanraja – or maybe I was also asking my crystal as well, because it could talk sometimes – *"or a possible thread of the future?"*

"It could even be happening now," Salanraja said.

"Hasn't the crystal told you?"

"Oh, I'm sure it would have waited for you to arrive before revealing anything important. If, that is, it's ready to reveal it now."

I growled. I honestly didn't like the fact that Salanraja had seen it first; I'd never quite accepted the fact that she could read my dreams, for that matter. Cats need their own private space, much as humans do. Particularly in such an unforgiving world, we need a place where we can be ourselves.

In the vision, Ta'ra emerged into the glade. She pounced

on the demon rat, and then the portal opened. Lasinta stepped out, displaying that wicked grin on her ancient, wrinkled face.

"*I guess you're saying that we need to report this to the Council of Three,*" I said.

"*Don't worry,*" Salanraja said. "*I've already done that.*"

The hackles shot up along my back. "*You did what?*"

"*I reported the dream to the Dragon Council as soon as you had it, Bengie. Then I reported it again when the crystal started displaying these visions.*"

The Dragon Council were just the dragons of the three elders who oversaw the running of Dragonsbond Academy. That made the Council of Three actually six in number – three dragons and three humans.

"*And why the whiskers did you do that?*" I asked.

I must have been snarling at this point. Salanraja had gone behind my back yet again.

"*You should be thanking me, Bengie. If we tell them immediately, you can't get in trouble for hiding it from the Council, don't you think?*"

"*Yes, but it should be my decision!*"

"*Correction, it should be* our *decision,*" Salanraja said. "*We are after all bonded. Or have you forgotten that?*"

"*If we're bonded, then I should at least be involved in the decision-making process!*"

"*You are. That's why I'm telling you about the decision now.*"

If I'd had dragon fire raging in my belly, I'd be breathing it right now. Salanraja had made me furious. I went over to the leg of beef and tore off a piece. I munched on it for comfort – it was juicy and soft. I retreated to the opening beside the crystal, and I lay down in a spot of sun.

Salanraja watched me, saying nothing about my diet this time – she didn't dare.

"*Anyway, we can fill this morning with more melodrama if you like. But I still thought you should know about this vision.*"

I turned my head back towards the image in the crystal, which had zoomed in on Ta'lon's smarmy-looking face and his plastic smile, while his yellow embroidered cloak swayed behind him in the breeze like a dog's tail.

I shuddered just thinking of him and the possible schemes he might be concocting with the warlocks. I'd never trusted that fairy, and I'd been right not to.

"*What are we going to do about it?*" I asked.

"*Well, the Council of Three has started to discuss the issue. They said that they'll report it to their superiors.*"

"*What? Ta'ra is in trouble, Salanraja, and all the Council can do is discuss it?*"

"*We don't know what this is, Bengie, and we won't until the crystals choose to reveal more.*"

"*I can tell you exactly what it is – Lasinta and Ta'lon are exploiting Ta'ra against her will, and we need to get over there and help her and put a stop to this.*"

"*Really? And how exactly do you plan to do that? You need a fairy in the Second Dimension to be able to open a portal. Do you know anyone who can do that for you, Bengie?*"

I racked my brain for ideas. "*What about the commune? The Cat Sidhe? Maybe Go'na or Be'las can help. After all they do owe us a favour.*"

"*You know full well that many of the Cat Sidhe have already used most of their eight transformations. If they use their final one, there'd be no going back for them.*"

It had been the evil warlock Astravar who'd turned them into Cat Sidhe in the first place. They all looked like regular cats, with the familiar cat smell, and a diamond patch of white fur on their chests amidst their black coats, which shone amber when the sun hit them. Because transformation magic always has an essence of impermanence, the Cat Sidhe had eight chances to turn back into fairies, and they could stay that way and use fairy glamour magic until nightfall. But once they had used up all their transformations, they took on the form of a cat forever. There was no way to undo that, much as Ta'ra had wanted to try.

Things hadn't gone so well for them since. They had tried to gain amnesty in the Faerie Realm, but that had been refused, so they had gone back to living like stray cats in the forest to the east. Driar Reslin, who supervised their commune, had reportedly announced to the king that they were suffering from a shortage of food. I had tried to get some time out to teach them how to hunt and feed themselves, but I'd been too busy with school.

"*Being a cat is not such a bad thing,*" I said, and licked a cluster of dandelion seeds off one of the markings on my fur.

"*For you it's not, but Ta'ra's a fairy who knows she'll never see her family again. You know what got her into this mess in the first place, don't you Ben?*"

"*The fact that she's a cat,*" I said. "*And she could never accept it.*"

"*No. The fact that she was once a fairy, and it's clearly impossible for her to go back, without the use of the wrong kind of magic.*"

"*Which is exactly why we have to put a stop to this.*"

"*It's impossible, Ben; that's what I've been trying to tell you. The Cat Sidhe can't open a portal on this side anyway, and besides this may not even be happening right now. We could be seeing a possible thread of the future that might occur if we don't do something. We have no way of knowing until the crystal chooses to reveal more to us.*"

I stalked back over and tore off another mouthful of beef, then returned to chew it in my sunny spot. I wasn't truly hungry – I was just eating because it made me feel better.

Outside, a flock of dragons on training exercises flew across the sky, and their shadows blocked off the sun for a brief moment. For that short second I couldn't see their colours, only dark silhouettes against the overpowering light. I imagined I could smell a whiff of rotten vegetable juice from somewhere, but I knew it was just my imagination.

I'd been in this situation before, but they said you had to be patient with the crystals. No matter what the stakes were, they decided exactly when to reveal crucial information and they were never wrong in doing so. But that didn't make it any easier as I watched Ta'ra's glowing green eyes, her wide pupils sapping the brightness away from them as she called out for help. My tail thrashed against the floor.

"*I guess we just wait, then,*" I said.

"*Exactly,*" Salanraja said. "*But I wanted you to know.*"

I stood up and turned back towards the doorway, because I knew there was still plenty to do. After all, I could already hear the commotion building up outside in the courtyard – because it was new school year at Dragonsbond Academy and the Initiation Ceremony was about to start.

4

THE WRONG TYPE OF GIRLFRIEND

Every single human resident of Dragonsbond Academy had gathered in the Central Courtyard. I made my way between the tangle of legs at the back, using my nose to sniff out a familiar scent.

Now that I was in my second year at Dragonsbond Academy, I couldn't stand right at the front anymore. This wasn't very practical for Esme, Max, and me of course, as we couldn't see over the heads of the human students. Fortunately we had human friends who could lift us over their heads.

I just needed to latch on to Ange's catnip perfume, or Seramina's snowdrop scent, or Rine's cheap musky cologne that he'd just started using. Alas, I didn't encounter them at first, but the more familiar scent of strawberries and cream. I looked up to see Bellari's red face framed beneath her curls of thick blonde hair. She was Rine's ex-girlfriend, and I'd once thought of her as my nemesis, until I'd convinced Rine to break up with her and start going out with Ange.

I hadn't annoyed her for a while, so I thought I'd have a little fun.

"Oh, Bellari," I said. "Could you pick me up please, Bellari? I want to be able to see what's going on up on the dais."

Bellari, who'd had a slight and dreamy smile on her face, looked down at me. Her eyes widened as she sniffed, and then her face went even redder.

Tears started to well up in her eyelashes, but they weren't tears of sadness. These were caused by 'allergies', although I'd always believed this was all in her head. Bellari never seemed to exhibit any symptoms until her gaze fell upon whatever she was supposed to be allergic to.

"I thought the Council had banned you from coming near me, Initiate Ben. You know it's not good for me."

"They can't control where I step," I said. "I am after all the famous Dragoncat, descendant of the great Asian leopard cat and vanquisher of warlocks. Now would you please help a Bengal out?"

"No ... you're a cat, and you know how it is. I'm allergic. Kamino, where are you – Kamino?"

She turned her head rapidly, looking for her new boyfriend.

"I'm here, darling," the Initiate said. He was big, with burly shoulders and a head shaved so close to his dark skin that it shone. He smelled tough, this guy. The kind of man you didn't want to get on the wrong side of.

"It's the cat ... he's harassing me, Kamino."

The boy looked down at me and smirked. "He's what?"

"You know I can't stand them. Honestly, now there's two cats and a dog here, and I'm always congested, and my eyes are so sore. I've complained to Daddy already, and he's asked the Council of Three to do something about it. Or at least he tells me he has ..."

She sniffed and the muscles scrunched up in her face.

"What? You're allergic to dogs too, now?" I asked.

"I'm allergic to animals, cat. And you know that."

"So you're even allergic to dragons?"

"No ... of course not. Kamino, *do* something." She wiped the back of her hand across her eyes, smearing off some thick mascara. "I don't want people to see me like this."

Her boyfriend had his arms crossed over his barrel chest and he peered down at me. "Haven't you got better things to be doing, Dragoncat?"

"I just thought that I needed a better view of the front. Say, you're big and strong, and you've got a good thick neck. Maybe you can put me on your head."

"Don't you dare, Kamino," Bellari said. "I'm not going near you if you get his fluff on you."

"It's not fluff, it's fur," I said. "The beautiful silken fur of the Bengal, handed down from the great Asian leopard cats throughout the generations."

"Whatever ... Kamino, don't just stand there ..."

Kamino shook his head slowly. He looked at his girlfriend so lovingly that it made me want to throw up. He turned back to me and pointed the toe of his narrow boot upwards.

"What big feet you have," I said.

"All the better to kick you with."

"You wouldn't dare. After all, I am the mighty Dragoncat, descendant of the great Asian leopard cat and the mighty Geo—"

He already had his boot off the floor, and Bellari had a wicked grin on her face not too different from the one I'd just seen on Lasinta's in my dream. Bellari had her hand clutched tightly around her boyfriend's. He had narrowed his eyes, which were deeply focused.

I didn't want to hang around to see if he would actually follow through. I scurried away, yowling in complaint. The students parted to let me through as I went off in search of a kinder crowd.

5

INITIATION CEREMONY

It wasn't long until I latched on to a whiff of the snowdrop perfume and began to follow it to its source. Seramina hadn't changed her scent, but she had started using a lot more of it. At fourteen she was now of an age where she wanted to fit in, and this was one of her ways of trying to do so.

Despite the scene I'd made back with Bellari and Kamino, the students had largely forgotten I was there. Thus I had to make my way between a forest of human legs – a real obstacle course for a cat, I can tell you.

I found Seramina wearing a knee-length bright orange skirt and a plaid olive-green jacket. She had certainly brightened her look since we'd returned from the School of the White, though admittedly she'd done nothing to change her long, straight, platinum-blonde hair. A cat scratch ran down her calf – neither Esme nor I had found out which of the cats in the cattery were responsible for that crime.

She had her staff strapped to her back, displaying a crystal that was white at its tip and purple at its base. My staff was the same, because now we Guardians of the White could use both white and dark magic. There was no point in trying to hide the fact that we were dark mages anymore – everyone knew. I tried not to use the darker form, naturally, not just because it smelled of rotten vegetable juice but because it could also consume my soul.

"Seramina," I said. "Can you please lift me up for a better view?"

She had her back to me, and as she turned her body slightly I saw she already had a white Abyssinian cradled in her arms.

"You're going to have to find another spot, I'm afraid, Ben," Esme said in the human language.

Esme and I were in fact the only non-human creatures here who could speak the language. She'd also received the special gift to speak the languages of all living creatures from the crystals, although I had no idea exactly when she'd obtained it.

I growled, feeling slightly betrayed. I would have been here far earlier if it hadn't been for the vision in the crystal – it would have been easy for me to find that spot. But Esme had sneaked in knowingly. Okay, I guess I was overreacting a bit, but then I was concerned about Ta'ra.

"Don't worry, Ben," Seramina said. "Rine and Ange are just over there."

She extended her finger to point over to the edge of the courtyard, but Esme meowed at her, so she returned to using her hand for stroking.

"Only one human per cat, Ben," Esme said. "You know the rules."

"Fine," I said, and went over to find them.

I rubbed myself against Seramina's calf before I walked away, so at least she'd retain some of my scent. Esme couldn't own this human entirely, much as I was sure she wanted to try.

Honestly, I hated having to deal with crowds – particularly human ones. We cats weren't meant for them, and as I dashed between the constantly shifting legs, the noises from the canopy of heads intensified. At least if I were up there, I could understand what the humans were saying. Down here, the voices melded together into one raucous storm, crashing against each other.

Of course, these were teenage conversations, and so they were probably talking about very uninteresting things like how pretty someone looked, or who might actually become a Prefect this year. Nothing about the quality of this morning's breakfast, and nothing about what is good for hunting and chasing around the academy this season.

I found Rine and Ange standing next to each other, just as Seramina had promised. They were holding hands, which I was proud to see. A blue-crystalled staff hung from Rine's back and a green-crystalled one from Ange's. I had been largely responsible for bringing this couple together, and once we were finished here in Dragonsbond Academy and had done our years of service riding dragons for the king, I planned to settle down with Ange and Rine in a country cottage. They could bring me lots and lots of delicious food, and I would spend my days happily chasing butterflies through the woods.

"I thought we agreed that you would spend your days in the cottage taking me on flights out to the mountains," Salanraja said in my mind.

Whiskers, I could never get used to her reading my thoughts like that.

"That as well," I said. *"But cats need to chase butterflies, just like you need to breathe fire."*

"And of course, I can roast you a different meal every day."

"Will you be quiet please, Salanraja? I'm trying to concentrate."

"Of course, you need to get a good view so you can see the new students. You want to know who they are."

"And you're curious too, aren't you?"

"I am, though the other dragons will tell me about it later."

That might be the case, but I wanted to know now. I meowed to let Rine and Ange know that I was by their feet. At first they didn't hear me, so I meowed louder. Rine also had his back turned to me. He wore long silken trousers and a black shiny leather jerkin, with a short-sleeved vest underneath it. His short, light hair tossed to one side as he turned his head towards me, and the features curved upwards on his boyish face.

"Ben! There you are. Ange and I were worried you might sleep the morning off. Though I'm not sure the Council of Three would have been too happy about that."

"I had important duties to attend to," I said, my head held high.

"What?" Rine replied, his eyebrows raised slightly. "Did Aleam run out of mackerel?"

"He has plenty of mackerel, thank you very much," I said. "But for now, it's none of your business."

"Suit yourself. Anyway, I suppose you'll be wanting a lift."

"That would be nice," I said.

Rine had developed some lithe and well-toned muscles in his arms, which I was sure could be used for lifting me fairly high.

"Only, you're going to have to ask Ange, I'm afraid," Rine said. "Today I'm taken."

"What, by who?"

I hadn't needed to ask, because the droopy-eared Sussex spaniel lifted his liver-brown head over Rine's shoulder and looked down at me with his wide dark eyes. Whiskers, I couldn't believe I hadn't smelled him over all of Rine's musk and the other masculine 'scents of the month'. Why did humans have to wear such ridiculous and unnatural smells?

"This boy is warm," Max panted in the dog language. "Dragon rider strong and cosy."

"Fine," I said.

I rubbed some of my smell off onto Rine's leg before I moved over to Ange. There was no way, if I was going to end up living with him, that I'd leave him permanently stinking of dog.

Ange's feet smelled strangely of her catnip perfume. Her toes poked out from her sandals, and she'd painted her toenails green. It wasn't just her toenails, though; she wore along, green frilly dress, a green blazer, and her fingernails were green too. She even had on green makeup, as if she'd decided to become a fairy herself.

I didn't question her about it, at least at first.

"Ange," I called, sniffing her feet. "I can't see from down here, Ange."

"Hang on, Ben," she said.

She was standing on her tiptoes, trying to get a view over the two lanky male dragon riders who were standing in front of her. Clearly I'd picked the worst of the humans as a vantage point. Now even Seramina had outgrown Ange.

"Please, Ange," I said. "It smells down here."

Ange turned her face downwards and then smiled kindly at me. "I'm sorry, Ben, I spilled my perfume on my foot this morning and didn't have time to clean it off."

"Meanwhile I can't see a thing."

"Right ..."

She bent down and scooped me up, then tickled me under the chin. I lifted my head. At least I could see something now of the crowd surrounding me, and not just their legs.

"Who's a pretty kitty?" Ange asked, and then she clucked.

"Not a kitty, a Bengal, a descendant of the great Asian leopard cat and the mighty George."

Ange shook her head. "That line never gets old, does it?"

"That's because it couldn't describe me better. Now what's with all the green?"

"It's traditional," she said. "I'm a leaf mage, and so I'm wearing the leaf mage's prescribed colours. It's an important day today, you know, Ben. We'll get new students, and then they'll announce the Prefects."

I scanned the courtyard to take a look at the other students. "But no one else is wearing their 'prescribed' colours."

Ange shrugged. "No one else cares that much. But can you see the front? At least the Driars are in their colours."

"You'll have to lift me a bit higher, Ange," I said.

Ange did as I asked, holding me as high as she could above her head. She only just managed to reach above the heads of the two lanky boys in front, and I could smell their hair cream.

"Do you see them, Ben?" Ange asked. "Only I can't hold you up like this forever. I'm not as strong as Rine."

Indeed I could. A couple of dozen Driars – or teachers, if you like – stood on either side of the raised dais at the front of the courtyard, and just as Ange had predicted they wore yellow, green, blue, red, and white. These represented their elemental schools – lightning, leaf, ice, fire, and shield respectively.

I couldn't see the Council of Three yet, but I could see our eldest and probably most respected teacher, the revered Great Driar Aleam. I knew him well, of course, given I slept in his workshop. He was dressed in yellow for lightning, even though he was in fact a dark mage. But that wasn't something you advertised in polite circles.

Above the dais hung the grand crystal. It was even

bigger than my and Salanraja's crystal, but not as big as the King's Crystal in the Tower of the Grand that Lasinta had touched with her staff not too many moons ago. It still displayed the cracks from when it had shattered into pieces after some powerful magic only a few months ago. Its facets were grey, displaying visions of the previous Initiation ceremony.

In the vision being shown on the crystal's facets, I recognised the red-haired student – the former Prefect Asinda. The crystal depicted her on the same stage, beneath the same Great Crystal, standing next to her boyfriend – the former High Prefect, Lars. But now they had both graduated as Driars. This was the title given to anyone who had completed their education at Dragonsbond Academy, with the title of Great Driar being reserved for Aleam and the three members of the Council of Three. The highest ranks in the king's Dragon Guard were also apparently Great Driars, but I'd never met any of them.

As Asinda and Lars had graduated and were now full-fledged dragon riders, they were officially serving the king. Earlier this year, the white mage, Captain Alliander, had tried to revoke Asinda's Prefect status and force her to study for another year. But King Garmin had reversed that decision, owing to Asinda's bravery in helping to save Bastet and the Fifth Dimension.

Since the celebrations of our victory, none of us had heard anything from Alliander. Despite knowing we were dark magic users, the White Mages had now left Esme, Seramina and me alone to be dragon riders. They were probably a little peeved at how we had learned to harness White Magic without needing a unicorn to serve as a channel. But that was just the way things were.

A tall object that looked a bit like a hat stand stood in the centre of the dais. It had six hooks around a central beam, in three pairs. The white crystal sat in a well at the bottom of this, currently grey and lifeless.

"Ben," Ange said. "My arms are really aching and I can't hold you up there much longer."

"Okay, okay," I said. "Lower me down. You can lift me back up when the students come to the front."

I can swear she almost dropped me, because her arms shook when a harsh grating female voice screamed out from the front.

A SPELL OF LEVITY

"Silence!"

The voice wasn't just loud and strident, but also old and wavering. It smashed against the voices of the students, shattering their conversations. It made me shudder in Ange's already shaking arms, and instinct made me want to leap out of them and scramble across the courtyard to safety. Cats aren't made for sudden loud noises, which is why we hate fireworks so.

The murmur coming from the students died to near stillness, with only a few trailing conversations hanging in the fray. Of course, Great Driar Yila – the owner of the loud grating voice – had been prepared for this. She was well practiced at using her voice to tame a crowd of adolescent humans.

"I said silence!" Yila shouted again, and then she stepped forward onto the dais.

This time, her scream washed over us like a tidal wave – as if a lion had just roared in our faces and we were staring it right in the face.

Yila was the oldest woman in Dragonsbond Academy,

being only slightly younger than Driar Aleam himself. Her face wore many wrinkles, most deep enough for fruit flies to navigate without crashing into her skin. She carried a staff with a red crystal on top of it, and she crashed the foot of it against the ground as if to subconsciously tell us what she would do to anyone who dared to speak again. Her eyes seemed to glow, but it was just the reflection from the red light that the crystal on her staff emitted. As with the other teachers and Ange, she had dressed herself in her uniform colours – a flowing red dress and matching robe.

She glanced back at the Great Crystal looming above her, and directed some of the red energy from her staff into the nearest face of the crystal. The moving images faded out of the mineral, and it started instead to glow white. The smell of burning charcoal drifted over from the front – which is exactly what fire magic smells like.

"A favour for the animals who are amongst us today," Driar Yila said. "Driar Lonamm, I think I'll need your help for this."

Whiskers, I didn't like the sound of this at all.

"Ange," I said softly, so my voice wouldn't carry towards the front. "You said you wanted to put me down."

"Hang on, Ben," Ange replied in the quietest of whispers, clearly knowing my ears could pick up on it. "I've heard rumours of this."

"Rumours?"

"Sssshhh ..." Ange said.

At the front, Great Driar Lonamm stepped onto the dais, wearing exactly the same matching dress and robe as Great Driar Yila, except this time in cyan. The stout and round elder stepped onto the dais, and she lifted her blue-gemmed staff, the crystal also glowing. This time, she fed a blue beam into the Great Crystal, which glowed even brighter and now pulsed with energy.

"We still can't do this alone," Lonamm said, her voice softer than Yila's, but nevertheless stern. "Great Driar Brigel, if you could also offer your aid?"

This was all a part of the show, I guessed. The teachers wanted to start this year with a lot of pomp and circumstance.

"Ange," I said. "Please put me down, Ange. I don't like this."

"Shush, Ben," Ange said. "You'll get us into trouble."

At the front, the Great Driar Brigel stepped heavily onto the stage. The Great Crystal cast white highlights onto his shiny bald pate. He didn't wear a dress like Yila and Lonamm, but instead green trousers and a green jerkin, and a long green cloak as well. He was dressed something like that human hero, Robin Hood, in the cartoons on television – the fox version of him, without the long snout and fur. But with his bulk, he more resembled his giant sidekick, Little John – if he'd decided to steal Robin Hood's clothing and swap the bow for a staff with a green glowing crystal on it.

"Happy to oblige," Brigel said as he lifted his staff. But before he cast a beam from it, he turned back to the audience.

"Oh, Initiate Rine ... and Initiate Seramina, is it? Yes ... could you please lift up your animals so they can get a better view?"

It was Max who complained about this first.

"What's happening? What's happening?" he barked, in the dog language of course. "Max not like this!"

I could also hear Esme yowling and screeching, and I was squirming in Ange's grasp as well, though I didn't dare use my claws. We didn't have very long to react though, because as soon as Brigel swung around with his staff and pointed a green beam at the crystal, a fourth beam emerged from the crystal proper. It was white and bright and quickly fanned out into three smaller rays, which found their targets on my, Esme's, and Max's foreheads.

I screeched aloud, but then a stillness washed over me, and I quietened down. My muscles suddenly relaxed, and the air tasted of that same kind of freshness you get after heavy rain. Esme stopped her yowling and Max ceased to growl. Beneath me, the shoulders of the students relaxed, as if our animal bodies were radiating waves of calm.

I eased myself into the embrace of the magic that wrapped around me like a shroud, and Ange released her grip on me. I didn't fall, because the magic from the crystal had me buoyed up and floating in the air, my legs dangling beneath me. It was as if someone had hung a hammock from a tree and straddled me over it.

"See, that wasn't so bad, was it?" Brigel called out from the front.

"We can't be weakening our human students just so the animals can see better," Driar Yila explained.

"Yes, magic is a much a better solution, don't you think?"

The three Great Driars shuffled around the stand at the centre of the dais, and they each laid their staffs horizontally on a pair of the hooks, so that they formed a triangle. The crystal at the base of the stand fed the crystals on the staffs with white energy, while the staffs fed the upper white crystal with beams of elemental magic.

Meanwhile, the three white beams were still split off from the Great Crystal, holding the three of us in place.

Now that their hands were freed, the three Driars turned to the audience of their students, and they gave us all a slight bow. The onlookers oohed and aahed in admiration, followed by a round of applause.

There I was, safe within a magical harness, the great Dragoncat floating above the other students without a worry in the world. But then a shudder washed over me as I remembered Lasinta, and Ta'ra, and the dream that had been or would become reality. On the breeze, I could swear I caught a whiff of rotten vegetable juice and my ears turned to what sounded like the distant wheeze of a condor and the heavy beating of wings.

Every warlock could turn into a carrion eater bird, and Lasinta's alternate form was a condor. I would come to regret my decision to stay silent, even blocking my thoughts in my mind from Salanraja, because the ceremonies were about to begin.

A WICKED SURPRISE

A raucous roar enveloped the assembly once again, coming from the students themselves. It made it hard for me to focus on the distant sounds of what might be the gathering schemes of warlocks. On the breeze came the smell of sweating students, and the manufactured scents they'd applied to try and mask their odour.

I hung above them, floating in a magical harness, fed by the beam from the Great Crystal on the dais.

"Okay, okay," Driar Brigel said. "That's enough now."

The bald giant put his arms out to try to silence everyone, but no one seemed to notice him.

"Silence!" Driar Yila shrieked again.

She didn't need her staff to enforce it; I swear, her voice could cut steel.

"Thank you, Great Driar Yila," Brigel said. "Now Aleam, the scrolls if you please."

Off-stage, Aleam picked up a box and handed it to Driar Brigel. It was filled with rolled up papers, each tied with a red ribbon.

"*What are they?*" I asked Salanraja in my mind.

"Initiation documents," Salanraja said. *"Every new student gets one."*

"Why didn't I get one?"

"Because you never attended an initiation ceremony."

"Does that mean I'll get one now?"

"Really, Bengie, what would you do with it?"

"I'd tear it to pieces with my claws," I said.

"I think the Council already know that," Salanraja said with a chuckle. *"Which is probably why you're not going to be a part of this ceremony."*

I growled, but in truth I didn't really mind. I'd much rather be floating up above the students without a care in the world than have to face the Great Driars on the cold hard stage.

What followed was intensely boring – so much so that I found myself yawning. I was so warm and comfortable in the embrace of my harness that I ended up drifting off.

In my dreams, I caught faint glimpses of my old feline *companion*, Ta'ra, in jeopardy in the Faerie Realm. Every so often I'd turn up my nose because I thought I'd caught a whiff of rotten vegetable juice. That would wake me up, but not for long.

In between naps I heard names being called out, and then I saw beaming students opening their rolls of paper at the front. They hadn't bonded with their dragons yet – that would come later, during another ceremony.

Then came the reading out of the Prefects, during which I probably kept my eyes open for a little longer. Ange was called out first, and Rine was called out as well. They both shuffled to the front together, though when they stood on the dais, they didn't hold hands. Bellari was called up as well, as was her tough boyfriend with the big feet, Kamino, but Seramina wasn't. I'd later learn of the Council's decision that although Seramina was the most powerful magic user to have advanced through the academy, she was simply too young to take on such a role. Esme, Max, and I weren't called up either. I was okay with that, though I was sure Esme, as the daughter of Bastet, would give me an earful about it later.

Every single Prefect on the stage gained a set of yellow shoulder pads to denote their rank. The Driars and Great Driars also put shoulder pads on themselves.

"Before we announce our High Prefect," Driar Lonamm said, "you must understand the duties that we assign to Prefects. They have a special role in Dragonsbond Academy, being next in rank to the Driars themselves, and we have selected them as role models for all the other students to look up to. Thus, you should see them as your superiors."

All baloney of course. Take Bellari as a case in point. I could look up to her alright, but only because she held her head so high that I ended up peering up her nostrils.

"If they ask you to do something, you should do it," Driar Yila continued. Each of them had a role to play – this had all been rehearsed. "We've also given them the responsibility to enact punishments. Should a Prefect find you stepping out of line, they have the power to ask you to copy out the Dragonsbond Academy school rules. You should take this not as an insult, but as an opportunity to grow – to become a better person and a better dragon rider."

"As Prefects ..." Driar Brigel began.

Above him, the Great Crystal flickered erratically. Brigel paused for a moment and looked up at it. A murmur rose from the crowd, and I felt my breath catching in my throat. Something was wrong.

"I said, silence!" Driar Yila called.

"Exactly," Driar Brigel said, and he chuckled to himself. "As I was saying, as Prefects you must always remember that you are role models in our society of students. You must – what in the Seventh Dimension?"

The murmur resurged in the crowd, and arms drifted upwards, fingers pointing towards the Great Crystal. The hackles shot up along my back, and to my side, where she was floating, Esme let out a deep growl.

The Great Crystal flickered again, and then it glowed brightly. A thin purple mist seeped out onto the dais. The stench of rotten vegetable juice pervaded the assembly.

A reedy and ancient voice resounded out of the crystal.

"You must always behave responsibly," Lasinta said, white light pulsing from the crystal to the cadence of her words, "and remember your oaths to the academy and the king that you took when you bonded with your dragons ... Such high and mighty language, which hasn't changed since the Council of Three were students at the academy themselves. Isn't that right? Order is established through rites handed down through the generations. No one ever questions what must change."

The three elders on the dais had been slow to work out what was happening. Driar Brigel spun around and faced the Great Crystal.

"It's the warlock!" he shouted.

The two women on the Council of Three spun on their heels to face the crystal.

Lasinta's wicked, wrinkled face watched out from all of the facets, like high-definition photographs. She seemed so close to us that we could see the hairs sticking out of the mole on her left cheek.

Brigel lurched for the magical stand in the centre.

"Oh no you don't," Lasinta said, the Great Crystal flashing white and the flow of energy from the staffs reversing, the beams turning purple. A faint yet visible shockwave pulsed out from the stand, throwing Brigel backwards. The giant bald elder fell to the floor.

"What are you up to, Lasinta?" Driar Yila said. "You have no place here."

"Oh, but it appears I do. Because I've been watching how you enforce order, screaming at the top of your voice. But see how silent the students are before *me*. Do something unexpected, and you gain rapt attention from a crowd."

While Yila drew Lasinta's attention, Lonamm crept over towards the staffs.

She had almost made it far enough to retrieve her staff when Lasinta turned her cruel gaze down upon her. She cackled loudly, and I could smell the fear rising from the students.

"Again you try to draw away my power," Lasinta said. "None of this shall work."

Another shockwave pulsed outwards, sending Lonamm reeling towards Brigel, who lay supine on the floor. She tripped up over his thick arm, and then crumpled over his body.

Meanwhile, Driar Aleam had organised the teachers into a line in front of the dais, pushing back the first-year students and the Prefects he had evacuated from the stage. The Driars at the front had their staffs drawn – a row of crystals glowing in different colours.

Lasinta's gaze roved over them, and her smile deepened. "Oh, Aleam, Aleam," she said, "the eternal enemy of the warlocks. The traitor who left us. What are you going to do now? Shatter the crystal – the most powerful asset you have in Dragonsbond Academy?"

Driar Aleam said nothing, but he continued to stand at the front, watching.

"*Is there anything we can do?*" I asked Salanraja. "*What's happening?*"

"*I don't know – nobody knows. Now hush, we dragons are talking. Trying to work it out.*"

My dragon's voice had such a sharp edge to it that I thought it better to leave the dragons be. Meanwhile, Lasinta's gaze within the Great Crystal roved upwards.

"Let's see, what do we have here," she said. "Some kind of magic."

Her gaze fell upon me, then I watched it drift further onwards to Max and Esme. She steepled her hands in front of her face, displaying five neat pairs of glowing purple nails.

"Gracious demons! Who'd have thought ... Three of my enemies trapped within a magical embrace. I could do what I like with you, but unfortunately I need you grounded for this fairy magic to work."

She lifted a hand and snapped her fingers. The warm magical harness released me, and I found myself screeching and tumbling through the frigid air. I hit the cobbles on my feet – naturally, being a cat – and then came the second flick of Lasinta's fingers, as crisp as a set of maracas.

My ears latched onto the distant calls of thousands of carrion birds, as they lifted themselves off their perches and screeched into the sky.

❧ 8 ☙

BIRDS!

I'd never heard birds cry so loudly, nor had I ever experienced so many approaching at once.

I couldn't see them, as I was trapped amidst the frozen legs of a good hundred or so students, many of them trembling in fear. But there was an awful lot of them, enough for me to smell the birds even at a distance.

They screeched and they cawed and they cackled, and I swear some of them even howled. I heard beating wings everywhere, drowning out the terrible sound of Lasinta's cackling laughter.

The noise from the crowd never rose above a murmur. Even when it did, Driar Yila didn't scream out to silence them. I really wished I could see what was happening in front, but all I could do was listen to the surrounding anxiety, my senses so incredibly augmented that I could almost hear every single pounding heart within the courtyard.

"*Birds,*" I said to Salanraja. "*We're being attacked by a whole massive flock of birds.*"

"*I can see that,*" she said.

"*Then why aren't you all out there breathing fire at them?*

Surely a flock of birds is no match for all the dragons in Dragonsbond Academy."

"*You haven't seen these birds,*" Salanraja said. "*There's so many of them, it's like a swarm of giant locusts coming from all directions.*"

"*It doesn't mean you can't flame at them,*" I pointed out.

"*We can't even lift ourselves off the earth – Lasinta's magic, it's keeping us all grounded. What's going on, Ben? How's she doing this?*"

I took another sniff of the air, trying to make out the magic amidst the smells of the teenagers. There was still the rotten stench of dark magic in there, and there was something else on the air, like honey that had just come out of the hive.

"*Fairy magic,*" I said. "*Whiskers, it's not just dark magic, Salanraja. This is why Lasinta needed those bags of fairy dust from Ta'lon; she was planning an attack.*"

"*Gracious demons, our crystal could have warned us about this earlier … or maybe that's what it was trying to do. We never listened … we never tried to see between the lines.*"

"*But what's Lasinta up to?*" I asked. "*What's she going to do to us?*"

"*No one knows, Bengie,*" Salanraja said. "*No one knows …*"

I didn't like this one bit. The situation set my whiskers twitching and my ears flattening against my head. I forced myself through the tangle of legs to Esme. I rubbed my nose against hers to comfort her.

Max was standing next to her, barking.

"Thousands of birdy wargs! Thousands of evil birdy wargs!"

"Birds are not wargs," I snapped back at him.

Max was in such a panic that he didn't seem to hear me. If we survived this, maybe one day I'd get a chance to introduce him to a real warg. For some reason, he thought everything was a warg but the wargs themselves.

"We should get out of the courtyard and summon our staff bearers," I shouted to Esme.

Our staff bearers were gigantic white hands that guarded our staffs for us. We called upon them when needed to place our staffs in our mouths so we could cast magic. This ability was unique to cats, as humans had hands of their own.

"No," Esme screamed back, the first time I'd ever heard her refuse a fight. "The birds would eat us alive."

She lifted her head and sniffed the air above her, but a student tripped on the cobblestones and her legs almost knocked into Esme. The Abyssinian dove out of the way just in time.

Now the screeches and the caws and the cries of the birds had drawn closer to us. My ears turned every which way, trying to assess the nearest threat. A shadow fell over Dragonsbond Academy – the flock above us, blocking out the sun. A sudden chill enveloped the courtyard.

At this point it was not only Max who was screaming, but everyone else as well, and at the top of their lungs. There was so much confusion that I only managed to pick up what was happening in bits and pieces.

"Everyone crouch down!" Driar Yila shouted. "Tuck your heads into your arms and brace. Do not try to cast any magic."

Aleam was also shouting something – I recognised his croaky voice.

Magic fizzled upon the breeze, but I had no idea who was directing it, or where.

Then Lasinta's voice seemed to rise louder above everyone else; it was like a foghorn finding its way through a swirling mist.

"Do not worry," she said. "I do not plan to take your lives. In fact, I think you'll much prefer your new abode."

Everything then seemed to close in on me at once. The

smells, the sounds, the brightness of the light, the sharpness of the shadows – it all rose up in a sharp crescendo. To my surprise, the birds didn't attack; instead, to my disgust, a deluge of white refuse plopped down from the sky.

As soon as the bird droppings hit the cobblestones, and the shoulders of the humans' clothes, and whiskers forbid even my beautiful silken fur, it rose up into plumes of golden dust. A purple cloud filled the courtyard, dispersing the gold outwards. The world grew even colder, and I thought we were about to freeze.

Then, everything fell silent. Time seemed to stop for a moment. A memory came back to me – a portal opening up in front of my bowl of salmon trimmings in South Wales and two coarse hands reaching out and yanking me through.

I felt myself suddenly accelerating, falling through time and space.

I tripped over my own front paw and fell sideways to the ground.

Other students also fell around me, but they did so silently. There was no sound in this place between worlds, which we now knew as the Sixth Dimension. Then the world seemed to crash against something solid and I found myself rolling across the ground.

Everything was still silent; not the sound of a single bird.

Soon enough my sensations flooded back, and they were much, much richer than they had been before.

9

ACROSS DIMENSIONS

I smelled it all – the honey upon the breeze; the blend of so many different types of pollen; the richness of fresh summer leaves; and the slight earthiness of the loamy soil.

The sky had a much more saturated hue to it, refracting all the colours of the land outside the walls of the academy. The students and Driars, who had been knocked to the ground, remained silent for a few moments. In the stillness, I could hear the sounds of chirping birds – not the horrific type that had just attacked the academy, but harmless sparrows and the screeching of a swallow. Bees and dragonflies buzzed every which way, and there came the rushing sound of a distant waterfall.

It took my brain a moment to catch up with my senses. I'm sure everyone else was going through the same hint of shock as they lifted themselves to their feet.

Then in a flash I worked it out. I had, after all, recently visited this place in my dreams.

"*Whiskers, we're in the Second Dimension,*" I said to Salanraja. "*The Faerie Realm.*"

"*No ...*" Salanraja replied, "*that's impossible ...*"

"Just look outside, Salanraja," I said. *"What do you see?"*

Salanraja hesitated. I imagined her walking over to the other side of her chamber so that she could peer through the opening to the outside world.

"Gracious demons, you're right, Bengie ..."

"Ben ..."

"Fine, Ben ... it doesn't matter. But the Faerie Realm ... how?"

There were enough students still rolling about on the ground that I could see over them to what was happening on the dais from my vantage point. The teachers had swarmed onto the stage to help the Great Driars to their feet. To the side, Driar Gallant — the castle's quartermaster – was propping up Aleam, the muscles on his arms shining with sweat. Above them, the crystal peered down at us with grey and lifeless facets. Lasinta must have drawn out whatever magic lay within it – at least for now.

Driar Yila found her footing first, and she strode over to pick up her staff. She examined it carefully. The crystal flashed bright red for a moment, then faded. Driar Lonamm and Driar Brigel also strolled over and picked up their staffs. Then the three elders raised their heads to examine the Great Crystal.

Driar Yila spun around and scanned the students in front of her. Though I couldn't see the details – my eyesight wasn't that good – I could still sense the sharpness in her expression. She was looking over the crowd for anyone who might have aided Lasinta.

Everyone was still picking themselves up and had started once again to murmur amongst themselves.

"Now, now, everyone remain calm," Driar Brigel said as he strode up next to Yila. "All students must stay in place as we assess the situation."

But I'd already decided I'd had enough. I wove my way

through the tangle of legs, picking up Salanraja's scent on the air currents. I found my way underneath the archway leading into the outer bailey.

I passed a guard in full armour standing underneath the tower, looking up at it. He was a regular castle guard, not a mage or a dragon rider. His breastplate shone brightly in the sun as I passed.

"Initiate Ben, is that you? Aren't you meant to be at the assembly?"

I turned back, and peered up into the huge nostrils of Onus, who was in fact the captain of the guard here at Dragonsbond Academy.

"I can't stop, I'm afraid," I said. "I'm on important business."

"Wait, wha—"

I didn't have time to hear the rest of the sentence, as I was already dashing towards Salanraja's tower and scurrying up the stairs.

"*What in the Seventh Dimension are you doing, Bengie?*" Salanraja asked.

"*Let's talk once I get to you.*"

"*But if you just run away from the assembly like this, they'll think you're complicit in Lasinta's crimes ... we'd be complicit, in fact, given you're bonded to me.*"

I let her words roll through my mind, not letting them slow me. By the time she'd finished her sentence, I was already standing underneath her giant talon looking up at her yellow eye. Her tail swished behind her, her body blocking the way onto her back.

"*Bengie?*" she asked. "*Are you listening to me? Return to the assembly at once.*"

"*No. Let me up, Salanraja. We're going to fly out and find out what's happened. We're taking matters into our own hands.*"

"*Really? And what makes you think we can just abandon our posts?*"

"*Because I'm the great Dragoncat, vanquisher of warlocks, and also one of Bastet's Guardians of the White.*"

"*You're also an Initiate of Dragonsbond Academy. Which means you cannot break the chain of command.*"

"*Salanraja, I know what I'm doing…*"

"*Do you, Ben?*" Salanraja cocked her head.

"*I…*"

I glanced at our crystal. Salanraja hadn't mentioned anything, but it was showing that same vision again, of Lasinta picking up the demon rat that Ta'ra had just hunted down. Ta'lon would be on the scene, and …

"*Salanraja, the vision. It is about to happen.*"

"*How do you know?*"

"*I just do … we need to get to Faerini now.*"

Salanraja let out a soft growl and lowered her head towards me. She got down so low I could smell the smoke coming out of her nostrils. But from the staircase behind me came a clank-clanking sound – Captain Onus no doubt, or one of the other guards coming up to return me to the assembly.

"*Fine,*" Salanraja said. "*I was never one for authority.*"

She turned around, displaying a path for me right up her tail onto her red scaly back. Over it, two rows of curved spikes towered upwards, creating an effect that looked a bit like an elephant's rib cage.

"*Well jump on, Bengie,*" she said.

I didn't correct her on my name this time; I didn't want to give her any excuse to change her mind. Rather, I clambered up her tail and nestled myself between two of her spikes.

My dragon lifted off into the air just as Captain Onus burst into the room with an expression of abject shock upon his face.

10

FLIGHT OVER FAIRYLAND

The first time I'd ever flown on Salanraja's back, I'd hated it. Back then, just after fleeing from Astravar's tower, I had encountered her in her chamber and unwittingly stolen some venison that she'd left out for lunch.

She'd then decided that instead of eating me, she would give me the aforementioned ride on her back. What I hadn't known is that she'd been waiting for me all along, because my crystal had revealed to her that we were meant to bond. But that is another story.

The flight that had followed that momentous occasion had absolutely terrified me; I'd thought that I'd tumble right out of Salanraja's corridor of spikes and into the mosaic of fields below. She'd flown erratically, and I'd given her an earful for her lack of grace.

Since then, flying had become easier. It was partly because I'd grown more accustomed to it. You kind of learned after a while how a dragon moves their body – it comes with being bonded, I guess. The more you learn to trust it, the more you mould yourself into their flight.

But Salanraja seemed to have also become more aware

that I was on her back. She would only perform a barrel roll or enter a sudden stall when she knew I'd prepared myself for it. So both dragon and rider had developed a sense of empathy for each other.

I had really started to believe that, until this flight through the Faerie Realm – because she didn't seem to want to keep me on her back at all.

"*Salanraja,*" I said in my mind. "*I feel sick. This is awful.*"

"*What do you mean, Bengie? I'm flying like I always do.*"

"*No you're not, you're turning more sharply and spinning all over the place and my body is getting bruised and battered from being thrown against your corridor of spikes.*"

I'd once likened it to like being stuck in a washing machine – which is exactly what it felt like, except of course without the hot water and suds.

"*I can't help it,*" Salanraja said. "*It's the currents in the air. They're different here; everywhere I seem to glide there's a thermal that lifts me up again.*"

"*You're lying,*" I said. "*You're flying badly because you're angry at me for taking matters into my own paws.*"

"*Really? Who do you take me for…*"

"*Just go easy on the barrel rolls, will you? I already had too much for breakfast.*"

Salanraja's laugh bellowed out through the sky. "*I never thought I'd see the day. The great Dragoncat, descendant of the 'great Asian leopard cat and the mighty George', vanquisher of warlocks, has eaten too much.*"

"*The way you say it, you make it sound stupid. Leave it to me to say. I know how to recite it properly.*"

Salanraja veered off to the right. I screeched and had to use my claws against her rough scales so as to not slide off her back.

"*Will you calm down, Salanraja?*"

"*But I thought we had to get there quickly?*"

"*Yes, but I'd rather get there alive …*"

A growl rumbled out from beneath my paws. "*Fine, I'll slow … besides, it looks like we've got company.*"

"*What? Where?*"

"*Look behind you, Bengie. I think you know that dragon.*"

"*Just stay stable if I'm going to crawl over to your tail.*"

"*Fine …*"

Salanraja levelled up so that I could look back. I saw a black dragon in the distance, but only a small one. A dwarf dragon by the name of Gratis, and I only needed to squint a little to make out the white Abyssinian sitting on his head, the wind tossing her soft fur back behind her.

"*Whiskers, does she ever leave me alone?*"

"*Gratis tells me that Esme isn't happy about you sneaking off like that.*"

"*How does she even know? You didn't tell anyone, did you Salanraja?*"

"*I hear that Esme lost your scent, and then she followed you all the way just to see you fly off.*"

"*So you must have told them where we are?*"

"*I never … it's a pretty clear day. It wouldn't have been hard for them to follow.*"

"*And she knows I'm going to see Ta'ra, no doubt?*"

Salanraja went quiet as she relayed my question to the other dragon. They all had the ability to talk telepathically amongst themselves, much as they could with their riders.

"*Wait, don't tell her that I'm going to see her if she doesn't know … it will only make matters worse.*"

"*Too late for that now,*" Salanraja said. "*But no, she didn't know. And you're right, it's just made matters worse.*"

It was ironic really; Esme had convinced me that I wasn't behaving like a true cat when I had considered Ta'ra my only *companion*. And now here she was feeling jealous, which was completely hypocritical.

Well, she-cats would always be she-cats.

"*About your flying,*" I said to Salanraja. "*Get there as fast as possible, Salanraja. Do whatever you need to do.*"

"*I thought you said my flying was making you nauseous. Because I don't want you throwing up on my back.*"

I looked behind me again to see Esme's staff bearer flitter back into oblivion. She must have summoned it when I was focusing on the sky ahead. Esme had her staff held firmly in her mouth and the crystal on it was glowing white.

"*What did you tell her, Salanraja?*"

"*Nothing,*" Salanraja said. "*I promise.*"

"*Just get us there as fast as possible. And lose them if you can.*"

At that, Salanraja let out a loud roar as though she wanted to split the air apart. But it wasn't a roar of anger – it was a cry of raucous laughter.

Then she dived downwards, and I held on for dear life. I felt sick again, but it didn't matter anymore, because I'd rather face a sore tummy than Esme's wrath any day.

SECRETS AND CONFESSIONS

Despite her best efforts, Salanraja didn't manage to lose Gratis or Esme from our tail. She might have done if there had been a single cloud in the sky for her to hide behind, but the sky remained clear and the sun beat down at full beam for the entire journey, as if it wanted to be personally present to welcome our sudden arrival in the Faerie Realm.

I still didn't want to deal with Esme, though. Salanraja had told me that she was angry, and there were few creatures in all the dimensions whose anger I feared more. She was after all the daughter of Bastet, and so she could probably curse me with having no fur and no claws for caternity. Or worse, she could send me to the fiery and sulphurous pits of the Seventh Dimension, to live the rest of my life serving demon Maine Coons.

Salanraja was near enough to the ground for me to work out a landing spot. I could see the glade in the distance, and against it a slight black blob on the ground, which I thought must be Ta'ra. Being a cat, I didn't have the greatest long distance eyesight. But fortunately, having twenty-twenty vision wasn't a requirement to become a dragon rider. There was no portal, or any sign of smelly dark magic, or warlocks or fairy princes. Right now Ta'ra was down there alone in cat form.

Still, I didn't want to land right next to Ta'ra – for one, I didn't want to be visible when Lasinta stepped out of the portal, and I also didn't want Esme there when I finally had a chance to see her again. I wanted the moment to just be between Ta'ra and me.

If only I could get there before Lasinta did, to warn her. Or to stop her somehow. Whiskers, I didn't know what I was going to do.

Next to the glade stretched a long field of lush grass, each long stalk glistening with dewdrops. *"Over there, Salanraja. Land in that meadow."*

"Are you mad? The grass is so long there, you won't be able to see where you're going."

"Exactly. That's how I'm going to lose Esme."

"Oh, and leave me to face her wrath? You're so kind."

"Just do it, Salanraja … or I'll summon my staff-bearer and use my magic to force you down."

"You wouldn't dare, Bengie …"

But my heart was pounding so hard in my chest, and I could feel something pulling on my muscles – a need for power, a need to stay in control. It filled me with such hope that I could almost taste that sweet dark magic upon the air.

"Just try me," I said.

And then there came a burning sensation at the back of my mind. A voice whispered so faintly that I didn't hear what it said, but I knew the darkness dwelled inside me if I needed it. I could use it to achieve what I needed to do.

There was a long pause.

"Fine," Salanraja said, after a while. *"But I don't like this. Something's off with you, Bengie."*

"*Ben!*" I shouted back at her in my mind. "*Now land!*"

She lifted her claws and dived down so fast that it sent me tumbling backwards. I continued to tumble down her tail and landed in a bed of soft grass. It smelled so fresh down here – even richer than the grass I used to run through in the valleys of the Brecon Beacons back home.

But then this *was* the Faerie Realm.

"*Don't tell Esme the direction I went in,*" I said to Salanraja.

"*Don't worry, I won't.*"

She didn't sound very convincing, but it didn't matter, because I had work to do. A cooling breeze rippled through the grass stalks, seeming to hang in their shadows. I lifted my nose, and I latched on to Ta'ra's scent.

She'd never smelled completely of cat, always keeping on her the faintest hint of lavender. Except now it was stronger, probably because she didn't want to smell of cat as a fairy. I found that insulting; I mean, what's wrong with smelling of cat?

Soon enough, I found my way through the grass and could see the blue of the lake and the sky beyond. Ta'ra was crouched there, ready to pounce on a demon rat.

I tried to leap forward and cry out for her to stop. Instead I ran into something invisible, which kicked me and sent me tumbling back. I growled as silently as I could and tried to step out again.

But this invisible thing was as solid as a tree trunk. I tried scratching it, and my claws felt as if they'd just glanced off leather armour.

Esme's voice came from behind me, sonorous and strong.

"Dragoncat, Dragoncat ... did you really think you could hide from a daughter of Bastet?"

I spun around, trying to see her through the grass.

"Esme, what the whiskers?"

Was it Esme, or was I imagining it? Because I couldn't see her, and I wouldn't be surprised if there was something in the pollen.

To my left I saw a flicker in the grass, and then a pink nose appeared out of the green. Esme's face emerged after that, then her shoulders, her body, and finally her tail which swished lazily above her. She still had her staff in her mouth, but now the crystal wasn't glowing.

"You've been keeping secrets from me, Ben," she said. "After the relationship of trust we've worked so hard to build – after everything we've been through together – still you feel you need to hide things from me."

I probably would have given a glib comeback to that statement under normal circumstances – after all, Esme wasn't the most honest of she-cats – but her sudden appearance had me awfully confused.

"Esme, how did you ..."

She let out a meow that in human terms would equate to a sigh. "I landed well before you did, Ben."

"You did what?"

"Really? You flew all this way and didn't even think to use a glamour. You have a lot to learn. Meanwhile, it's obvious you came here to see Ta'ra. She's in her cat form, I see."

I twitched my whiskers. "You don't sound particularly angry."

She stalked up to me and sniffed my face. She still had the smell of mackerel on her breath.

"Why would I be angry, Ben? Because you snuck away without telling me where you were going? Or because you've come here to visit your former *companion?*"

I took a deep breath and blinked hard. Then I told her as much as I knew – after all I had nothing to lose now that I'd been caught red handed. I told her about the dreams, I told her about the visions in the crystals. I also told her that

Lasinta had probably been sourcing fairy dust from this realm in exchange for helping Ta'ra keep her fairy form – working in league with Ta'lon.

Esme kept her ears pricked while listening, and the expression darkened on her face.

"And you wanted to hide all this from me? Why?"

"Because I'm still thinking about Ta'ra, and you're my *companion* now ..."

Esme uttered a meow that wasn't a sigh this time, but a chuckle. "Really, Ben, you think I'd mind?"

I blinked. "Don't you?"

She brushed past me, angling her staff so it didn't hit me on the head.

"Just come on," Esme said, "let's see what Ta'ra and Lasinta are up to."

Before she went towards the clearing, she used her staff to cast a glamour upon us all – including both dragons – to ensure we were concealed from view.

12

THE DARKNESS BEYOND

Just as we reached the edge of the meadow, a purple glow arose over the landscape to my left. There came that disgusting stench of rotten vegetable juice, and the portal winked into existence out of nowhere. It shone as a white halo in front of us, offset against a row of shivering alders and casting a second radiance in the reflection on the water.

The land beyond the portal was dull and grim, permanently covered with a blanket of sheer greyness. I'd only been to the Darklands – the abode of the warlocks – a few times, but still I shuddered to look at it. It was a lifeless place, comprised of stark rocks and magic.

The horizon glowed purple, framing a mass of white wispy creatures lurking on the barren ground, pushing away the shadows. I knew these beings well, because Salanraja and I had fought them many times before. They were manipulators, servants of the warlocks, each of whom could cast dark magic from their spectral staffs.

If the warlocks had their way, every landscape in every single dimension would look this way. There would be no life at all, and hence no food for a mighty Bengal like me to eat, only creatures of dark magic that existed for one single purpose – the immortal reign of the warlocks.

I'd thought for a while that we'd beaten them when we defeated Astravar, and we'd stopped the rise of this evil force that powered dark magic, known as *Cana Dei*. Then we'd defeated the Warlock Prince, Arran, and the *Cana Dei* that had consumed him. Again, for a short time, I'd thought we'd won.

But great lulls of peace always seemed to follow such cataclysmic events, as if life were a series of anti-climaxes leading one into the other. Now Lasinta had teleported Dragonsbond Academy to the Faerie Realm, and we had no idea why. Yet it seemed the scene that my crystal had predicted was finally about to happen.

She and all the other warlocks may have thought that they could resist *Cana Dei*, that it wouldn't eventually destroy their minds. They were wrong of course, because *Cana Dei* eventually works to suck the souls out of its users until they become its mindless servants. Now that Seramina, Asinda, Esme and I could all use dark magic, we had to be incredibly careful.

Which is why we four Guardians of the White had all vowed never to use dark magic except when absolutely necessary.

"Whatever you do," Esme said, as if reading my mind, "do not run in there and try to stop this. We need to assess the limits of Lasinta's power."

She sat next to me, her body still and her brilliant blue eyes focused on the portal. In front of me Ta'ra was on her haunches, waiting. The demon rat lay inert in front of her. I sniffed the air for traces of Ta'lon, but I couldn't detect him. Either he wasn't here or he had glamoured the scent out of him, and I didn't know which.

Lasinta stepped out of the portal. Her eyes turned downwards, and that wicked grin was again displayed on her face. She stooped down to pick up the demon rat, and then came the words that I'd heard in my dream.

"Thank you once again, dear fairy. You shall have your wish, and I shall have mine."

Her eyes crinkled, and more purple smelly mist came up out of the ground. Lasinta's crystal began to glow. I knew what was coming next – the beam would hit Ta'ra and turn her into a fairy, and she would lose her will.

I couldn't let it happen. My crystal had shown me this possible future for a reason. I had the power to change our destiny, much as I had done numerous times before.

I summoned the magic from within. Power surged into my body and my muscles began to feel numb. Then I was yowling and roaring in pain, as I willed myself to transform. To summon the chimera within, much as my crystal had taught me to do many moons before.

"*Bengie, don't!*" Salanraja said in my mind.

But I wasn't listening. I mean, who could blame me? I'm a cat, and I'm impulsive; it's in my nature.

My bones tore out of their joints, to be replaced by a fresh, newly grown skeleton. My muscles stretched and the pain became more intense as a second head grew out of my neck and a third one out of my tail. Thick fur spouted from my mane, and soon enough I was letting out another yowl, which became a bellowing roar.

I tucked my lion's head into my chest and lowered my goat's head, facing the horns forwards. Then I charged, my snake's head tail hissing and whipping out in the air behind me.

13

CHARGE OF THE CHIMERA

My giant lion paws scuffed the ground in front of me, and my rear goat hoofs kicked up even more earth behind. My four limbs windmilled along the ground as I gained momentum. I planned to ram Lasinta head on, and she wouldn't know what had hit her. All the while, I kept the fangs on my snake's tail bared, dripping with venom.

A cooling breeze whistled off the lake to my right, and the reflections of the distant rolling hills rippled in the corner of all six of my eyes. But they were focused on just one target.

My efforts would end the life of another warlock before she'd had the time to operate her evil schemes. The Dragoncat of legend would once again be a hero.

Alas, it wasn't meant to be ...

"You!" her voice boomed out ahead of me, the air seeming to crackle in its wake. "Why are you attacking such an innocent old lady?"

Just as soon as Lasinta had spoken her voice seemed to block my path, because I crashed into a wall that felt like rubber and bounced right off it again. A thick plume of smelly purple gas rose into the air in front of me. I tumbled back across the ground, lion's paws and goat's legs and snake tail getting tangled up with each other.

Lasinta had her staff pointed right at me. She cocked her head to one side and then she uttered, "Well, what a surprise this is, Dragoncat. It's a pleasure to make your acquaintance once again. How have you been doing since our little reunion in the Tower of the Grand?"

For a moment she actually sounded genuine – as if she really were happy to see me here, despite my attempt to toss her over to the other side of the lake. But I knew that she had to be faking it, and so I growled in my deep guttural lion's voice. Then to add extra special effects, I bleated out a goat's cry followed by a terrifying snake's hiss.

Lasinta didn't budge an inch.

Meanwhile, my heads were splitting. If there's one thing worse than a headache, it's three headaches in all three of your heads at once – there are certain disadvantages to being a chimera.

I called upon my staff bearer and it lunged forward to place my staff within my massive jaws, the crystal at the top glowing in anticipation. I wasn't sure whether I wanted to use dark or light magic yet, though given the way the power of the staff was calling me, it would probably be dark.

"Oh no you don't," Lasinta said, and a red beam shot out of her staff towards the giant white hand.

Before it could impact my staff bearer, it vanished safely into thin air. It had an automatic defence mechanism, it seemed, for which I was thankful, because I didn't know what I would do without it.

It was at that moment that Ta'ra seemed to awaken from whatever hypnotic magic Lasinta had used to ensnare her. "Ben," she said, "what are you doing here? Lasinta, don't harm him, he doesn't know what he's doing ..."

The sunlight glinted off her green eyes as I turned towards

her. For a moment, the white diamond crest on her chest also seemed to shine brightly in the light.

Though she very much looked like a feline, she smelled much more of lavender than she did of cat. The air seemed to glimmer with a faint golden sheen around the edges of her, as if a fairy aura wanted to cling to her fur. But she couldn't hide who she truly was – or at least what Astravar had turned her into.

"I'm here to rescue you," I said. "Lasinta is using you for her own purposes. She's turning you into a fairy against your will, and she's stealing fairy dust that she intends to use to accomplish evil deeds."

"It's hardly stealing if I've brokered an agreement," Lasinta said.

"Shut up! I'll deal with you later," I said.

Lasinta narrowed her eyes. Yet there was still a hint of something in her expression that I hadn't seen before. Could it have been kindness? If it was, then Lasinta was surely acting, because she was anything but kind.

"Oh, I don't think you will." The wrinkled warlock twirled her staff in her hands. "I need to protect all of us; I hope you understand."

"You will do him no harm," Ta'ra said, "or the agreement is off. You know how this works."

"And who are you to make decisions?" Lasinta asked. "Where's your beloved prince Ta'lon now?"

"He's running a little late," Ta'ra said. "But he'll be here."

"Yet here I was thinking we'd agreed on the utmost necessity of timeliness in our transactions. It's important for the smooth running of things."

A smooth male voice trickled out of the space at Ta'ra's side.

"I'm here," Ta'lon said, and a golden cloud manifested out of thin air. A human form developed from it – a familiar and handsome man with high cheekbones and oiled black hair.

"Glad you could make our meeting, Ta'lon," Lasinta said, her foot tapping as she turned her head back and forth between him and Ta'ra.

Ta'lon exhaled a breath he'd clearly been holding. "You wouldn't believe how much politics I have to deal with nowadays."

"I'm afraid you know how these things work ..." Lasinta said. "Time cannot wait for politics."

"That is where you are mistaken, Lasinta. Given that it's Faerini who is supplying the product, it follows that we should be the ones who set the terms, and time passes differently in the Faerie Realm than it does in other dimensions."

That certainly seemed to be the case. In fact, I'd go so far as to say it was the one thing that cats and fairies have in common. We have no respect for deadlines; we abhor them, in fact.

"We'll have to see what your king says about that," Lasinta said.

"I'm afraid that my father has left me in charge of all negotiations; he can't stand the stench of warlocks."

Lasinta turned her shoulder as if ready to leave. "Look, do you want your wife to be the perfect representation of a fairy, or not? Because you can't do it alone, remember? You can glamour her all you like, but without dark magic you cannot mask her smell at court. What will the other fairies think, Ta'lon? Your fellow royals ... your father ..."

Lasinta's face twisted as she spoke the final words, and for a moment I saw her innate cruelty return to her, brought about by a lifetime of using dark magic. The moment was indeed brief, before a normal calm expression once again washed over her face.

"I've tried everything," Ta'lon said, shaking his head

slowly. "But Astravar's magic is just too strong. We can't mask it all."

"Of course you can't," Lasinta said. "Because you haven't been trained in the magic of warlocks. But that's exactly what I'm here for."

Ta'lon gave her a slow blink, his eyes screwing up tight as he did so. Just before they did, I thought I caught a flash of something reflected in them. Something abnormal and evil, although I couldn't place exactly what.

Then he turned his head towards me as if noticing me for the first time.

"Well, if it isn't Ben the Bengal. What are you doing here?"

"I came to stop you from giving Lasinta that fairy dust and to stop Ta'ra being turned into a fairy against her wishes."

"I'm sorry ..." Ta'lon said, and his eyebrows furrowed.

"You heard me. Ta'ra doesn't want this."

"How would you know what I want, Ben?" Ta'ra snapped back. "This is what I have to do aid the realm."

"But you asked me for help," I said.

"What? When?"

She certainly didn't sound happy to see me – even though it had been so long since we'd seen each other.

"In my dream ..." I twitched my whiskers and my heart sunk in my chest. "You mean to say you want this? You cannot trust her."

"Well I never," Lasinta said, one hand on her hip. "I'll have you know that I've reformed. After seeing what my grandson went through, I couldn't possibly follow his example. No more dark magic for this old warlock."

"Yeah, so what did you just throw at me?" I said. "That was dark magic you just threw in my path."

"You forced me to act on instinct," Lasinta said. "I had no choice."

The whites of her knuckles were showing on the hand which clutched her staff as she studied me, probably trying to work out whether I'd try to take her down once again.

"Yeah, so what do you want with bags of fairy dust?" I said. "And why did you transport Dragonsbond Academy to the—"

"Is fairy magic not better than dark magic?" Lasinta cut in before I could make my second accusation. "Because all we warlocks have ever wanted is to use magic without consuming our souls."

Whiskers, where had Esme got to when I needed her? I really wasn't any good at this diplomacy stuff.

All if in answer my to call, a sudden sound cracked like thunder right next to me, causing me almost to leap out of my massive chimera hide. The air split, and I caught a sudden whiff of ozone.

Esme flashed out from her hiding place in the grass, and her blue eyes glowed as she cast powerful white magic at Lasinta. But the beam didn't hit her, because Ta'lon clicked his fingers as soon as he saw Esme appear.

The beam welled up into a ball halfway in between Esme and Lasinta, and then there came a poof of golden smoke. A white goose stood in the place where the magic had converged. It turned its yellow beak towards Esme, gabbled, and then waddled off.

I watched it narrowly, feeling suddenly hungry.

"No unauthorised magic in the Faerie Realm," Ta'lon said. "Particularly against an ally of Faerini."

"An ally?" Esme hissed the words out of her mouth, speaking in the human language but still sounding incredibly cat-like. "This is ridiculous. You cannot trust Lasinta. She's our mortal enemy, and not far off from being a mindless servant of *Cana Dei*."

"Prejudices, prejudices," Lasinta said. "Can an old

woman not reform? Especially after what happened to my grandson ... I don't want to end up like Arran. None of us warlocks do."

"Exactly," Ta'lon said. "Lasinta is on our side now, and you've still not told us what you're doing here in the Faerie Realm in the first place, *Dragoncat*."

Something about the way he used my fabled name didn't sit right with me. I'm not sure I'd heard Ta'lon use it before; only the warlocks and the crystals seemed to use it with any regularity.

Esme opened her mouth, as if to explain to Ta'lon how Lasinta had somehow used the fairy magic that he'd been supplying to her and a great flock of trained birds to bring us all here.

But she didn't have a chance and neither did I, as there was a crackle in the air, and another golden plume of smoke emerged next to Ta'lon. Out of it stepped a plump man, wearing a red silk robe and carrying a gnarled oaken cane – no crystals on it – and wearing a wreath bespeckled with berries on his head.

"King So'ta," Lasinta said. "The ruler of all Faerini. To what do I owe the honour of your royal presence?"

The fairy king got straight to the point. "Nothing to do with you, I'm afraid. It's about these two creatures ... traitors to our kingdom."

He gestured at us with his staff.

I wanted to shout out at him that we were no such traitors. Last time we'd visited Faerini, we'd gone to see the Oracle Fairy – who wasn't in fact a fairy at all but a giant ash tree – and she'd helped us to defeat Arran. But something had sealed all three of my mouths shut. Esme also looked as if she had golden thread sewn through her lips. Magical fairy thread – which meant it was probably a glamour.

But powerful fairy glamours didn't just trick the eyes into

seeing, they tricked the mind into believing something was there. King So'ta, I'd heard, was one of the most powerful fairies of them all.

No one had physically sewn up our mouths with golden wire, but that didn't matter because it kept our mouths shut in any case. Fortunately So'ta wasn't cruel enough to also make us experience the pain of such a thing.

"Now first," So'ta said, "you, Dragoncat, can return to your normal form."

He pointed his staff at me, and in a golden flash I was a beautiful Bengal again. I hadn't felt any sensation during the transformation; I simply was a chimera one moment and a cat the next.

"And as for the glamour – really Ta'lon, you need to learn to be more observant if you're to be king."

"I don't understand, father," Ta'lon said.

"Oh, you will ..."

So'ta swept his staff around again, and our dragons appeared, standing in the fields. The grass barely concealed the red scales on Salanraja's talons. She completely dwarfed Gratis, who had his dark head lowered as if he wanted to hide himself in the grass.

I tried mumbling through my lips, but none of the fairies seemed to hear any of it. Neither did Ta'ra, who was just staring at Lasinta now, her eyes glazed over as I'd seen them in that dream.

"Father ..." Ta'lon said.

So'ta raised his hand. "You know the rules, son. We will not tolerate King Garmin's dragons coming into our realm without express written permission from the fairy consuls. This is an act of war."

"That's if they remain in our territory," Ta'lon pointed out.

"Yes ..." So'ta replied, and he put his free hand on his chin and then glanced at Lasinta. "I see what you're saying. We shall then leave them under the jurisdiction of Queen Ca'mun."

Lasinta gave him a nod, as if to give the fairy king permission. He swept his cane around once again and cast out more powerful fairy magic. In an instant, Esme and I and our dragons flickered out of existence.

But this was only temporary.

Unlike the act of travelling through portals, I felt nothing during the teleportation. We presently found ourselves lying on the cold cobblestones that lined the outer bailey of Dragonsbond Academy.

I picked myself up and recalled what I had just experienced in that scene, and indeed it was troubling. Just before So'ta had cast his magic, I had seen a glint of purple in the eyes of Ta'ra, the fairy king, and the fairy prince. A glint, in other words, of dark magic, which wasn't a good thing at all

…

ABYSSINIANS AND DESTINY

The outer bailey, and the inner courtyard beyond it, had completely emptied out. There was not a soul to be seen, not a cat from the cattery or even a swallow or a starling, as if the very birds of the Faerie Realm thought it best to stay away from this place.

The sun had already reached its apex in the sky, and was now starting its slow descent towards the horizon. Still, it was blazing down pretty hot. Perhaps that was one of the reasons everyone had retreated indoors – they were afraid of getting sunburnt. As far as I knew, no one had invented sunscreen in the First Dimension, although admittedly leaf mages like Driar Brigel and Ange could summon plants out of the ground that would provide a soothing shade and make the air smell of fresh spring.

Once, I'd seen a whole dozen of them working in tandem under the tutelage of Driar Brigel to build a ten-foot oak out of nothing. Then, because I love climbing, I'd dashed up to the high branches and sat there and watched the world go by for a whole afternoon, and no one had done anything to get me down.

Brigel had scolded me later that evening for missing some classes, to which I'd replied it was his fault for putting up the tree in the first place. I am a Bengal, descendant of the great Asian leopard cat, with claws and muscles designed for reaching great heights. This is probably one of the reasons I ended up bonding with Salanraja and took to flying – it was in my makeup.

Let's just say that Driar Brigel hadn't seemed very impressed by my explanation. I got detention for that evening and the evening after, which was fine because I ended up just sleeping through both of them. Anyway, I digress ...

I meowed without saying anything meaningful, happy that the horrible magical thread that had previously bound my mouth closed had vanished. I could hear dragons growling in their chambers in the towers above us. Speaking of which ...

"Salanraja, are you okay?" I asked.

"I think so," Salanraja said. *"No broken bones, and King So'ta didn't turn me into a goose or anything. Yes, my wings look normal, and I still have twenty claws."*

"Glad to hear it," I said. *"And I'm well too, thanks for asking."*

"I know ... we are *bonded, you know."*

"Well, it's still nice to have a little compassion sometimes ... to have my dragon asking the obvious question. It goes like this: 'how are you, Ben?'"

"Bengie," Salanraja corrected – or at least she tried to.

"Ben ... my name is Ben!"

Salanraja didn't have anything else to say to that, but it didn't matter because I had already picked myself up off the floor. I headed over to Esme, who was grooming grass pollen off her fur, and rubbed my face against her pink nose.

"Thank you," I said.

"Why?"

"Because you weren't angry about Ta'ra, and you helped me with the situation in the first place. You were right to come ..."

Esme meowed softly, and then she gave me a slow blink. "I didn't mean *what* are you thanking me for, I meant why are you thanking me in the first place?"

"What do you mean?"

"I keep telling you, Ben – you're a cat and I'm a cat, and we don't need to thank each other for simple things. Save that for the humans, to help them feel better about themselves, but only if it helps you get what you want."

"Fine," I said. "Well at least you smell of cat and not of lavender."

Esme cocked her triangular head. The sun beating down on her made it glow at the edges. Really, I'd never heard of an Abyssinian having such white fur, but then I hadn't met many of her breed.

"So does that mean you're over this nonsense with Ta'ra?"

I lifted my head. "What do you mean, 'nonsense'?"

"Your feelings ... they're very human and not becoming of a tom."

"So you keep telling me," I said.

"That's because it's true – and you never answered my question."

I hesitated. "Yes, I'm over it. I am over Ta'ra. I don't have any human feelings for her—"

"*Liar,*" Salanraja said.

"*Shut up ...*"

"*Fine.*"

"*I mean, Ta'ra did virtually blank me. It was as if she didn't care that I was there.*"

"*Didn't you want me to shut up?*"

"*Yes.*"

"*Doing so ...*"

"Fine—"

Suddenly, it was as if my dragon had decided to cut me off from her mind. I could no longer feel the dragon fire burning at the bottom of her belly, or the slight sensation of scales pulling at her skin.

She'd once told me never to do that; to always keep the bond present. Every time I'd blocked her off from my mind, she'd been so angry with me, as if it wasn't okay for a cat to want a little bit of privacy. But I wasn't so sensitive about it; I had told her to shut up after all.

I gazed off at the fountain in the distance. The water had stopped flowing from the stone fishes at the top of it, but then, I guessed it had lost its source.

"You know," Esme said after a moment, "I'm a very intuitive she-cat, and I can tell that you're lying to me."

"Why are we even talking about this?" I asked. "We've just been teleported into the Second Dimension by a flock of screeching glamoured birds that were clearly fairies, then we go over and try to find out what happened – to stop Lasinta doing what she might have done to Ta'ra – and ..."

"You saw it too?" Esme's eyes narrowed.

"The purple glint ... yes, so it wasn't just my imagination. Lasinta's done something to those fairies, Esme. She's done something to Ta'ra."

"It seems that way. So the question is, what are you going to do about it?"

"Usually, it's you who has the answer to questions like that, Esme."

"Well, you are the mighty Dragoncat, descendant of the great Asian leopard cat, are you not? It's time that you started living up to your heritage."

I growled at her again, this time right from the base of my throat, not liking the implication that I wasn't living up to my ancestors' legacy. My ears perked up, and I listened for a moment to the murmuring coming out from the dormitories. I caught a whiff of Sussex spaniel on the air, accompanied by the musty scent of desert cheetah.

I latched on to it, and edged towards it slightly as I focused on the direction of the scent.

"We're going to find our friends," I said.

"That's the spirit," Esme said, and she gave me a slow blink and once again rubbed her nose against mine. "Take the lead, just as you're destined to do. Believe me, you've not yet touched the surface of what you will become, Dragoncat."

Whiskers, why wasn't she angry with me? It was as if she was always scheming, always trying to mould me into the image of what she thought I should be.

I mean, it was only natural that I wouldn't appreciate this. Every cat wants to be his or her own individual, the master of his or her own destiny. But the way Esme behaved, it was as if she thought she held my destiny in her own paws.

And here I was, accepting her as my *companion*. Sometimes – often in fact – I felt like I didn't even have a choice.

"Come on, then," I said.

I stalked off towards the dormitories, not once looking over my shoulder to see if Esme was following behind.

DORM ROOM MEETUP

The dormitory rooms have no windows, and so the students tend to leave the doors open, to let in the natural light from the gothic windows in the corridor that looks out onto the outer bailey. Esme and I stalked along this corridor, appreciating the sunlight shining through.

Three students, a cheetah, and a dog had gathered in Rine's dormitory room. It looked no different from the first time I'd been in there. I had slept in here once, right underneath the single trestle table that lay against the far wall. A wide beam of sunlight passed through the open doorway, and so the tallow candle on the table remained unlit.

It still had my scent there, that I had marked underneath the table. I had intended that as my litter spot when I'd first set foot in this room, just in case Rine had decided to lock me in here. Fortunately for Rine, I'd never had the chance to use it.

Rine and Ange sat at the foot of the single wooden bed. Ange's head rested on Rine's shoulder. Seramina had plopped herself down at the pillow, her knees tucked in towards her with a dusty book resting against her legs. Max lay by the wardrobe, fast asleep.

Ange's pet desert cheetah, Palimali, surprisingly had curled up next to the Sussex spaniel and was also asleep, breathing gently. She had come here from the Sahara in the Fourth Dimension, and she had told me numerous times that she hated dogs. Which meant she must have recently learned to tolerate him – but with Max we all did eventually.

Motes of dust danced in the sunlight as I waltzed into the room. They swirled in an eddying motion, and I watched the way they framed Esme standing in the doorway for a moment. My interest didn't last long, and so I turned my head to the bed and meowed, half forgetting why Esme and I had decided to come here in the first place. Then – because of all the dust – I sneezed.

Rine lifted his head. I didn't understand it; everything just seemed so calm in here. So much so that I thought I'd better go with the flow, just in case my friends had also been taken over by warlocks or something.

Admittedly, on our walk to the dormitories my sense of urgency had also washed out of me. No doubt this was the fairy magic playing with the threads in my mind – trying to rewire them until I forgot what had happened entirely. I couldn't let it.

"Well, look what the cat dragged in," Rine said.

"You've used that line before, Rine," I said.

Rine paused. His tongue seemed to stick in his cheek for a moment. He glanced at Esme.

"Well, I was going to say another cat, but you kind of spoiled it."

"How about he brought in a brilliant alabaster Abyssinian," Esme said, her head held high, "her fur shining brighter than the reflection of a full moon in a silver lake on a cloudless night."

"That right there," Rine said, pointing a finger at Esme. "What was I telling you, Ange? Now Esme's starting to sound just like Ben with his 'descendent of the great Asian leopard cat' malarkey. Except she's somehow managed to make it sound poetic."

Esme's annoyance at Rine's comment ran so deep beneath her fur that I could smell her anger. Admittedly I understood her; no cat likes being told that they aren't special in their own right. The good thing for most humans is that their cats don't understand what they say to them. Because if they did, humans would walk around with a lot more scratches on their calves.

"An Abyssinian is a far more special breed than a Bengal," Esme said. "Everyone knows that."

I hissed at her and bared my teeth. No words needed to be said; Esme had just turned it completely on me. She was a complete traitor to the feline cause.

"See what I mean?" Rine said. "Just like Ben ..."

"You know, funnily enough," Seramina said from her spot by the pillow, "I'm reading about Abyssinians right now."

"Why, what are you reading?" Rine asked.

Seramina showed him the cover of her book. It was green, with a picture of a cat that looked like a miniature version of Bastet but without the torc around her neck, traced out in golden foil.

"It's a bestiary of ancient and magical cats. The Abyssinian is in here on page one-hundred-and-sixty-seven."

"One-hundred-and-sixty–seven?" Esme said. "I should be on page one."

"No, page one is Bastet, and then there's the chimera, and the lynx who stalks the Third Dimension. The 'Hellcat' of the Seventh Dimension, one of whom Ben crushed to oblivion against Lars' shield. The Beast of Bodmin Moor, whatever that is. And there's another entry from the Fourth Dimension near the back – the Cats of the Alhambra."

I mewled happily to hear this. Out of all of the breeds Seramina had mentioned, the cats of the Alhambra were the most fabled amongst our clowder back home. Cats often went on pilgrimage to the Alhambra – which we knew as the centre of the world, or at least my home in the Fourth Dimension. There you could find cats from all over the globe – well-travelled cats full of fascinating stories. The old Ragamuffin in our neighbourhood had in fact once journeyed to the Alhambra, which was why he was so wise.

"So, what about the Bengal?" I asked. "What page am I on?"

Seramina shrugged. "Sorry, Ben. From what I've heard, you're quite new to the game. I only found one mention of the Bengal, and that was under the section of a more recent cat breeder by the name of Mary Jean."

"Never heard of her," Rine said.

Seramina glanced up at him. "Anyway, Esme, it says here that Abyssinians are perhaps the oldest domesticated cat in the Fourth Dimension, and they think you might have migrated together with the earliest humans there. Something about a place called Ethiopia?"

"Fascinating," Ange said.

"But I've never heard of Ethiopia," Rine said.

"You've not heard of much," I pointed out.

"Why, have you?"

"As I matter of fact ..."

There was something in the tales of the Savannah cats back in my home country. I had found it a riveting story, and I'd even gone on to retell it a few times. But at that moment I couldn't recall it, and that irked me a little.

"Ben?" Rine asked.

"Yeah, I have had ... I've heard of Ethiopia. Of course ..."

Esme still had her head held high, her nose sniffing the air above her. "Ethiopia is my ancestral land," she said. "Of course it's only natural that we should look after the humans; they tilled the fields to feed the livestock that supplied us with food, and all we needed to do was make sure no scorpions slept under their pillows."

Seramina laughed. "Good bargain, I guess. But say, it also says you come in four natural colours – ruddy, blue, sorrel and fawn."

"There's more colours than that," Esme said.

"Yeah, it mentions a few more mixes, but still no alabaster white. So where do you get your colour from, Esme?"

"I'm a daughter of Bastet," she said simply.

"Whose fur is as black as moonless midnight," I pointed out, because I could do 'poetic' too. "So surely it can't be in your genes."

"I'm not a literal daughter of Bastet, you fool," Esme said. "I was born in the Fourth Dimension, just like you. But Bastet pulled me out more years in the past than you could possibly imagine. Time doesn't flow in her Fifth Dimension – the World of Souls – like it does in other realms. In your terms, I must have lived thousands of years."

"That still doesn't explain why you're white."

"It's because of the White Magic," Esme said. "I've used so much of it over the years that my fur couldn't possibly be any other colour."

"Like unicorns?" Ange asked.

"Yeah, like unicorns ... if you like." Esme wrinkled her nose.

I didn't like where this was going. I've said it before, and I'll say it again – unicorns are nothing better than decorated horses. They smell like horse, and no horse can be trusted. Every cat I've known has said to stay away from horses.

You try and get close to a horse and they'll kick you in the face. Wisdom like this has been passed down from one cat generation to the next for a reason – it had kept us alive.

"Okay, so what's been going on since we've been gone?" I asked.

Rine looked first to Ange, and then to Seramina. In the corner, Max lifted his nose to the air, sniffed, then placed his head back down on the floor and gave a deep growl. A cold draft blew through the open door, coming from the windows outside.

"We're in lockdown," Ange said after a moment. "But not to worry, this is all a drill."

"What do you mean, a drill?" I asked.

"Oh, you didn't hear?" Rine said. "That whole business with Lasinta was staged. They wanted to test us, to check that the academy can respond to emergency situations."

He looked at Ange. "It's a protocol that King Garmin has ordered the academy to perform once every seven years. It keeps the teachers in check, makes sure that the syllabus is spot on. We performed well, and so they've given us the rest of the day off."

"Without being able to talk to our dragons," Seramina said, shaking her head.

"Yeah, we've been cut off from that too," Ange said. "All a test to see how we respond, to see if we're able to react well in situations like this without panicking. Because it can happen sometimes that the bond is broken – in extreme situations – and we need to learn to manage by ourselves."

I blinked in disbelief, my whiskers twitching like butterfly wings. Clearly the Council had lied to them, but I was having to rack my brain to remember the truth.

"Speaking of which," Rine said, "the Council of Three wasn't happy with the two of you. After the staged catastrophe, they did the register and you two didn't answer your names. Where did you both run off to all of a sudden?"

The answer should have been on the tip of my tongue. I struggled to push a memory to the front of my mind, as if I were fighting to the surface in deep water. I saw green grass, red scales, a crystal-clear lake. I saw green eyes looking at me with a glint of purple in them, a portal looking into an even purpler land, a wreath bespeckled with berries on a fairy king's head. But I couldn't attach any meaning to these memories.

"Salanraja," I said. *"Salanraja, something's wrong."*

She didn't answer. But then Ange had said that we had been cut off from our dragons, and we weren't meant to panic.

"You do realise that we're in the Faerie Realm, don't you?" Esme said, and I could see a knowing look that I didn't quite understand in her eyes.

Seramina looked at Esme for a moment. She gave her a quizzical look, then turned back to her book.

"Don't be silly," Rine said. "We didn't even pass through a portal."

"Must be part of the test," Ange said. "They've brought Esme in on it too."

I wasn't liking this, but I didn't know why. We were in the Faerie Realm all right, I remembered that now that Esme had mentioned it. I remembered the assembly, a panic, the Great Crystal glowing white and a wicked and cruel face upon it. But who did that face belong to? I didn't know. And why could I remember the stench of so many birds of prey?

There came a rapping at the door – the sound of metal tap-tap-tapping against wood – ever so lightly.

A female guard with black curly hair stood in the corridor, her armour blocking off the sun so that the front of it looked dark. I smelled fear, and could see the worry on her face. Not the kind of worry that comes from a physical threat, but rather of trying to remember exactly why you were here.

She had a scroll in her right hand, which she lifted to her face and unrolled. "Initiate Ben and Initiate Esme of Dragonsbond Academy," she said. "You have been summoned to the Council Chambers and must attend immediately."

She lowered the scroll and took a deep breath, and she stared blankly ahead of her.

"They took their time," Esme said, and she picked herself up and strode forwards with some urgency.

I knew it was best to follow her, even though I found myself wondering exactly why.

16

DISSOLUTION AND CONFUSION

I followed Esme into the tall square tower that rose high above the courtyard, my nose and my legs guiding me because my brain had no idea why I was there. Cloisters ran around this courtyard, surrounding a massive patch of freshly cut grass that smelled slightly dry after being roasted by the high, burning sun.

The sensations that I felt were all somehow familiar – the texture of the cobbles against my paws, the puckering of the skin underneath my fur, as if it was recalling the memory of being recently stretched, of a bond inside my mind with a creature that I knew I needed to reconnect to. Yet I had no idea why these sensations were important; I had no idea of where I actually was.

Meanwhile, my mind was trying to sift through my memories – trying to work out the chronology of events, which felt like trying to find gold in dredged up silt. I saw a bowl of salmon trimmings, two harsh male hands yanking me through a cold portal – or was it warm? – a black cat with a white diamond on her chest turning to me and asking for help. Who was she? I had no idea.

Each time an event rose up in my head, I had no way of connecting it to the others. I was becoming lost inside my own mind.

We entered the tower – the Keep Tower, yes, that's what it was called – and we had entered from the Inner Courtyard. But why were those places important? What meaning did have they have in my life?

The door had three coloured crystals set into its centre – green, red, and blue. When I looked directly at them, they seemed to glow. But that had to be my imagination, surely? Crystals couldn't glow.

A white cat with a pink nose sat down next to the threshold and scratched at the door. I knew this cat ... she was an Abyssinian. Yes, that was it – an Abyssinian. But were Abyssinians usually so white?

She looked at me with her two bright blue eyes, and as I looked back into them they seemed to almost glow. But cats' eyes always glowed in the right light, didn't they? And who'd ever heard of an Abyssinian with such bright blue eyes?

"I should have seen it earlier," she said. "It's already happening."

"What is—" I had the question on the tip of my tongue. But all of a sudden, I couldn't remember what I wanted to ask.

"Tell me, and tell me now: who are you?"

"I'm Be—" My name. A human name, wasn't it? But why was I speaking in the human language to another cat? I continued in the cat language ... or was it the human language? In all honesty, I wasn't quite sure.

"I'm a Bengal, a descendant of ... a Ben – my name ... Ben."

The cat before me narrowed her eyes. She was white, and she was an Abyssinian. I'd encountered Abyssinians before, but I'd never known one of these strange cats, with their ears almost as big as their head. Pink inside the ears. Hairs sticking out. A cat, a white cat. She was white ... so white ...

"Ben, yes your name is Ben, and you're a descendant of the great Asian leopard cat and the mighty George. Remember that."

"My name is ... Ben," I said. "My name is Ben, a descendant of the great Asian leopard cat and the ... descendant of the—"

"Descendent of the great Asian leopard cat and the mighty George," the white she-cat cut in.

"Yes, the mighty George. The mighty George. I know him ... he's important ...."

"Good," she said.

What was her name, was it Ta'ra? Salanraja? Was she the old Ragamuffin? Surely it wasn't the feline way to call other cats by names. We only needed to identify them by their breed. So why would I think this cat had a human name?

"Now do what I do," she said. "Whiskers, what kind of spell did So'ta cast? We can't let the fairy magic wipe everything out of your mind."

The white cat, the Abyssinian, closed her eyes. All of a sudden, there came a flash of white in the air and a whiff of freshness. A gigantic white hand appeared in the air above the white cat. It was bigger than the biggest bird I'd ever seen, and it held some kind of wooden rod in its grip with a white and purple crystal at the end.

It flew downwards, tracing an arc that made me think it was going to whack me with the staff. I dashed back into a corner, screeching. But the hand hadn't intended to attack, but instead it placed the weapon – whatever it was – between the white cat's lips.

"Do what I do, Dragoncat, descendant of the great Asian leopard cat and the mighty George."

I stared at the white cat blankly. I should know her, I

knew I should. Now she was telling me to summon a hand that flew out of oblivion. But why should I trust her? I mean, any normal cat who met another cat with those abilities on a dark night would soon be running for the nearest bush.

Better if the bush were catnip – I remembered that much. I liked catnip, and I also liked hot smoked salmon. In fact, smoked salmon was my favourite food. Also, my tummy was rumbling. I couldn't remember the last time I had eaten, but I could taste some kind of fish on my breath.

"Close your eyes," the white cat said, "and summon your staff bearer, Ben ..."

"My staff ... my what?"

"Your staff bearer. Whiskers, Ben, you're a lot further gone than I realised. Hang on, this may sting a little."

The crystal glowed white on her strange rod, and a beam of white light flooded out of it. It hit me on the forehead and warmed my skin there, and then my brain also warmed inside my skull. A memory surfaced at the back of my head.

A giant white hand, and the knowledge of how to summon it. All I needed to do was pluck it out of nothing. It sounded so simple when I put it like that, except it was simple to pluck something out of anything – but to remove something from *nothing*, in the language of mathematics burrowed deep in my brain, that would make a negative something. But you couldn't have negative something – or at least you couldn't look at it with your naked eyes.

Why was I thinking about mathematics, anyway? Speaking of which, where had I learned such a nonsense language? No one ever spoke in mathematics, did they?

"Just do it!" the she-cat said. "Stop thinking about it."

I growled, and I knew I didn't have any choice. I closed my eyes, and I saw the image of a crystal – a giant crystal, tall and long, with shiny white facets, spinning on its longitudinal axis where it hovered in thin air. On its facets there was a cat

with amber fur and dark leopard-like spots holding a staff —
yes, it was called a staff – in his mouth.

That cat looked familiar. But then of course it looked
familiar, because I'd looked at the same cat in the water – my
reflection. The cat was me.

And with that vision I started to remember ...

I willed power to my mind, and then I opened my eyes to
see that a gigantic white hand had appeared just in front of
me. It held a staff with a white and purple crystal that I knew
to be familiar. I didn't even need to call upon it, because in
one clean swoop it lunged forward. My jaw clenched onto the
haft, and the staff began to burn with energy.

"Now, Ben," the white cat said. "You need dark magic to
nullify fairy magic. There is no other way."

Her name ... Esme ... yes, her name was Esme. The magic
was telling me that much. In fact it told me much more than
that; it called to me, like a seal singing from the arctic waters,
or an owl hooting into the void at night.

I clenched down on the staff, and warmth flooded
through me. That soon became a burning sensation that
surged from the back of my tongue down to the smallest
muscles in my paws.

"*Embrace me,*" said a voice in my head. A voice I'd learned
to fear – the voice of *Cana Dei.*

"*Your days as a free one are numbered, because eventually I
convert all warlocks to my cause. You are mine, now, Dragoncat. You are mine ...*"

From all around me rose the sweet scent of dark magic. I
could taste it on my tongue. I could lick it off the air.

Purple gas seeped out from the cracks between the
cobblestones. My muscles burned even more – every single
muscle in my body. But the sensation wasn't unpleasant; it
filled me with power. I was more alive than I'd ever been, as
wild as wild can be.

My memories flooded back to me, and I saw long stalks of grass everywhere around me – tendrils of dark magic reaching out of the ground. They shivered in the dark breeze, and I could feel them reaching out to me, curling towards me as they filled me with dark energy. The power to destroy worlds and unite the dimensions. The power for everything to be as one – a unified conglomerate. No need for individuals anymore. Power. Power. Power—

"Ben, stop," Esme said. "That's enough!"

A flash of white before me, and the tendrils of darkness disappeared. For a moment, I was surrounded by nothing – the Void, a vision of the Eighth Dimension where everything eventually ended up. The River of Souls flowed into it, carrying the sediment deposited by our souls in slow eddies towards the ultimate end.

I blinked. Once. Twice.

I saw spots before my eyes, then I saw the double oaken doors that led to the Council Chamber in Dragonsbond Academy. The familiar crystals that locked the doors – and only a few in all the dimensions knew the magic to open them.

Esme stood in front of me. Esme, the brilliant Abyssinian, my *companion*. How had I forgotten her? Whiskers, how much had I forgotten?

The fairy magic had tried to steal it all away.

Esme shuddered in front of me. It wasn't a shudder due to cold, but one of a wave of fear passing over her spine.

"Despite Bastet's best efforts to cure you," she said, "I fear you've passed too far over to the other side."

"What do you mean?" I asked.

I could feel how wide my eyes were in my sockets as I took in everything around me.

"Like Seramina, you must be careful of dark magic. I

hadn't thought it possible, even though Bastet told me she was afraid for you."

"Afraid for me? Bastet?"

I remembered her now – our immortal guardian. But why would she be concerned about me?

"Just don't use dark magic unless it's absolutely necessary. I can't watch over you twenty-four hours a day, Ben."

I nodded, then I turned back to the door, because there had come a voice from behind it. A powerful yet croaky voice. Driar Yila's …

"Is it safe now?" she asked. "Have you controlled him?"

"I have," Esme said.

"Then you may enter," Driar Yila said.

The crystals glowed all three of their respective colours, then the door creaked open narrowly enough to let a concentrated beam of white sunlight stream through.

"Hurry up," Driar Yila called. "Because we don't want to let in all the fairy dust."

17

FAIRY DUST

The three Great Driars sat behind their desks in the Council Chamber, the sunlight coming through the three windows behind them, silhouetting their forms. They still wore the same ceremonial robes they had worn for the assembly, but the colours didn't look so vibrant in this light.

But then, nothing from the First Dimension could look vibrant against the colours of the Faerie Realm. It was as if the Second Dimension carried a wider spectrum of colours.

Different patterns of stained glass adorned each window behind the Great Driars. My head was still spinning from having almost lost my memory to fairy magic, so I had to squint to make out the shapes in the windows. I had never truly looked upon them before.

Driar Yila's window showed a female dragon-rider on a red dragon and in a red cloak, casting out burning swathes at a field of fire golems, fury burning in the mage's eyes. The fire golems themselves looked like tiny flames on the ground, but I knew how dangerous they could be once they hit their targets, creating intense explosions that consumed everything around them, sucking up all the oxygen in the air.

Driar Lonamm's window displayed a female ice-mage on a blue dragon, battling an army of spectral manipulators. A thin icicled beam had shot out of her staff to knock out the crystal heart of one of her enemies – exactly what we'd had to do when we battled them.

Driar Brigel's window displayed a male leaf mage flying on a green dragon, casting streams of vines from his staff in an attempt to subdue a forest golem. I'd encountered forest golems on my adventures – great whirlwinds around a central crystal, which sucked in the natural material around them. Eventually they could gather enough compacted branches and leaves and mulch to become formidable foes.

Most striking about all three windows were how the mages they depicted looked exactly like the three members of the Council of Three, except as much younger versions of them. Which meant the dragons in each window were the dragons of the three elders – Farago, Flue and Plishk.

Salanraja had told me many times how she feared all three of these dragons. In all honesty, I wouldn't want to have to fight them either. Without my staff I wouldn't stand a chance – even in my chimera form.

The light from each window created red, green, and blue beams that met at a massive crystal in the centre of the chamber. This focused the light into one white beam that fed the tri-colour crystals on the door.

Since I'd last been in this chamber, the Driars had tidied their desks. They probably saw how I had examined each one, looking for a possible trinket close enough to the edge to knock off with one of my errant paws.

Now, only a single black goose feather quill teetered over the edge of Driar Yila's desk. I examined it with delight for a moment, imagining it in my paws. But then I saw Driar Yila's glare and decided this might be a test. Besides, quills had ink on them, and I didn't want to get any of that yucky stuff on my fur.

Esme strolled forwards and positioned herself just beside the crystal in the centre of the room.

"You summoned us," she said.

"Yes," Driar Brigel said. "Yes, indeed we did."

Driar Lonamm stepped around from her desk and moved towards me. She bent down to examine me. I felt suddenly hungry, and meowed in response. Usually when someone crouched down like that they were about to give me a kitty snack.

"He looks safe," she said, and picked herself up. "You did a good job, Esme."

"Of course I did a good job," my feline *companion* replied. "I've had more than a lifetime's worth of training from Bastet."

"Meanwhile, would someone please fill me in on what's going on?" I asked. "Because right now it seems no one knows where we actually are. Do you even know it?"

Driar Yila sucked in a breath. "We're in the Faerie Realm, we know."

"You do?" I asked.

"They do," Esme said. "They managed to lock themselves in here before the fairy dust could affect their minds."

"Whiskers! This doesn't sound good at all. You'd all better start explaining, because I've had enough of everybody's secrets."

Driar Yila almost jumped for her staff hanging on the stand behind her. "Don't you dare speak to a Great Driar like that. I should ..."

Her voice trailed off. She didn't seem to have the energy to do anything at all.

"It's okay, Driar Yila," Driar Brigel said. "We've all been

through a lot. Meanwhile, Initiate Ben, allow us to fill you in – because I'm sure neither you nor Esme of the White know the full extent of the events that have transpired today."

The story the Council of Three told me was alarming, and that was putting it mildly. They had heard rumours from their dragons — who'd learned about it telepathically from King Garmin's own dragon – about an imminent attack from the warlocks before that day's assembly. But no one had known exactly when it might occur, or where the warlocks might strike first.

What they hadn't realised was that Lasinta had managed to ally with the fairies. It turned out that it wasn't a flock of carrion birds that had flown over our assembly at all, but fairies glamoured to look like them. Only fairies could open a portal to the Second Dimension, and they had sprinkled enough fairy dust over Dragonsbond Academy to transport the entire castle across the dimensions.

The residual fairy dust then worked to cut off the bonds between the dragons and their riders, and also to affect the dreams and memories of any creature within the castle. All you had to do was breathe in the stuff, and it got to work on your mind.

Therefore, as soon as the Council of Three had realised what was going on, they'd locked themselves in this room from which they could make decisions on how to proceed. Aleam had apparently also locked himself in his workshop. But without access to their dragons, the three elders had no way of knowing if the fairies had managed to get to him too.

For all this magic, there needed to be fairies near to the castle controlling the spell. Problem was, the fairies would had glamoured themselves invisible. They must also have glamoured the fairy dust so it didn't have its usual golden sheen.

As the elders spoke of fairy dust, I lifted my paw and

examined the bottom of it. Indeed, it had a gold residue sticking to the paw pads, looking like I'd just stepped in a pile of sticky glitter.

It also had a specific scent to it – much sweeter than dark magic – sweeter even than honey. This was the first time I'd ever heard of fairy magic being used for evil purposes, and I told the Council exactly that.

"We've never known anything like it," Driar Lonamm agreed. "And never has an event occurred like this in history – or at least to our knowledge."

I had placed myself in the shade of the mantelpiece, next to some smoky, charred logs of firewood, untouched since the winter. I wondered if the Council of Three had ever roasted anything within the rough-cut stones, because this wood would add a wonderful taste to fish.

"Initiate Ben, are you listening?" Driar Yila asked.

"I am, ma'am," I said. "It's just that I'm awfully hungry."

"Didn't Aleam give you breakfast?"

"He did, but I transformed into a chimera when we encountered the fairies, and I'm always ravenous when I turn back."

The room went silent except for Esme's deep growl – her pupils two narrow vertical slits – just like the daggers she was glaring at me.

"We know quite well where you've been," Driar Yila said. She drummed her fingernails over her desk.

"You don't sound particularly angry about it," Esme said.

"Well, did you not have instructions from your crystals?"

I chirped, happy that Salanraja and I had probably got away with this. Technically, our crystal had not told Salanraja and me to go, but after the dreams and the visions, I'd just known it was the right thing to do.

Esme said as much: "Initiate Ben had a dream. And I had visions too, and so I knew I had to follow him."

"Her guardian," Driar Lonamm said. "Always so loyal."

"And so, what did you see?" Driar Yila asked.

I decided it was best to tell them the whole truth and nothing but the truth, even though I knew they weren't going to like what they heard …

18

QUESTIONS OF AUTHORITY

Light streamed continuously through the windows of the Council Chamber. It seemed to flicker to the rhythm of my voice, almost as though it were laced with magic.

I told the Council of Three everything – how Ta'lon had apparently brokered a deal with Lasinta to stop Ta'ra from smelling of cat, and how I had turned into a mighty chimera and tried to attack her, but her senses had been too sharp – almost as if she'd been expecting me there all along.

I also told them about the purple gleam that I'd seen in the fairies' and Ta'ra's eyes, and then I went back even further than that.

What followed caused the Great Driars to cock their heads with interest, looking like three identical replicas of each other.

I went on to tell the story of how, when we were studying at the School of the White to become White Mages, Captain Alliander – our tutor and Arran's half-sister – had confiscated our staffs, fearing that we may all lose ourselves to *Cana Dei*.

But we had gone to recover them from the Tower of the

Grand, which housed the King's Crystal in the top of the turret. This was the largest crystal known across all the realms, and it singlehandedly powered the magic in Cimlean City, among other things.

It was a grand heist indeed. We'd even recruited the King of Cats in Cimlean City and his army of moggies to distract the White Mages so we could get inside the tower. In exchange, Seramina and Asinda had cooked up the grandest feast of mutton sausages ever, so delicious that the smoky scent of the food had managed to push away the stench of the midden outside our shack hideout in the slums.

But even though our plan had seemed perfect, the White Mage, Carmista, had managed to foil it and she'd nearly managed to magically teleport us back to the School of the White where Alliander would have handed out severe punishments. That was when Lasinta had shown up, apparently saving the day.

We had met the elderly warlock outside the tower, and she had understood why we needed to retrieve our staffs and thwart Arran the Warlock Prince's attempt to release *Cana Dei* across every single dimension. Esme had then used her white magic to remove the barrier surrounding the King's Crystal. Lasinta had touched her staff to the crystal, and transformed into a condor and flown out one of the tower windows towards a silver full moon.

Esme kept her gaze narrow and pointed at me, like two pins boring into my skull, but she didn't try to stop me telling my tale. When I had finished, she turned her head towards Driar Brigel and said, "Well, what do you think?"

Driar Brigel folded his muscular arms and shook his head slowly. "Most alarming ..."

"You should have come to us with this information much sooner," Driar Yila chimed in.

"Indeed," Driar Lonamm said.

"But it didn't happen during school hours when we were living in Dragonsbond Academy," I pointed out. "In fact if I recall, we were studying at the School of the White at the time."

"So did you tell Captain Alliander?" Driar Yila asked. "Because at that stage she was meant to be your ward."

"Ward?" Esme laughed out loud in a very catlike way. "We are not children."

"Still, the issue remained unreported to anyone in authority," Driar Yila said.

"I was the authority," Esme said, and she took a lick of her fur.

Driar Lonamm exhaled a heavy breath. "You are no authority – you are a cat, and a very haughty one at that."

"I'll have you know that I have plenty of authority. I have lived much longer than any of you, and my authority comes from Bastet herself."

"Yet you didn't send it up the chain of command," Driar Yila said. "King Garmin needs to hear of such things. We have structures in place to ensure it reaches him."

"I told Bastet," Esme said.

"Bastet is no good to us," Yila said. "As long as you're serving under King Garmin, you need to take measures to ensure information flows up towards him."

I was getting so angry with the council that I was tempted to knock that goose quill off Driar Yila's desk after all. If I timed it just right, I could get the ink to splash right over her robes. I readied myself to pounce.

"What are you doing, Initiate Ben?" Yila asked suddenly.

"I ..." I rose. "We don't have time to be assigning blame right now."

"He's right," Driar Brigel said. "We need to work out exactly what Lasinta is up to."

"Obviously she's managed to somehow gain the ability to

control fairies," Esme said. "It must be a new gift, because otherwise she would have used it a long time ago. The question is, how is she doing it?"

The room went silent for a moment. A mote of dust must have found its way up my nostril, and I tucked in my nose and sneezed. Everyone turned their heads to look at me, as if they thought I might have the answers. But honestly, other than perhaps the woodlice that I could see crawling beneath the logs in the fireplace, and the mouse that I could hear scurrying behind the walls, I was the most clueless creature in the room.

"It's a forced gift," Driar Lonamm said abruptly.

"A what?" I asked.

Lonamm looked at Yila, and at Brigel. Then she turned her gaze downwards towards Esme and me. "There's a good reason that Garmin ordered a ward spell cast to surround the King's Crystal and protect it from any users of dark magic. It is the crystal from which all gifts are derived. Before any crystal can grant a gift, they first consult with this crystal. The King's Crystal, I've heard, has the power to warp time and space, to create a reality that can accept any newly granted abilities. I believe that Initiate Ben here has received a few of such gifts."

I lifted my head up high, suddenly feeling proud. "Of course. I have the gift of being able to speak the languages of all creatures in all dimensions, as well as the gift to be able to transform into a mighty chimera."

"We know, Ben," Esme said. "There's no need to repeat it."

"I'm just—" I stopped myself, realising that I was allowing us to get side tracked. "Are you telling us, Great Driar Lonamm, that Lasinta managed to steal a gift from the King's Crystal?"

"Not only that," Yila said, her voice laced with concern.

"A warlock who comes into contact with that crystal can use dark magic and the power of *Cana Dei* to take any gift of her choosing. She only needs to define clear and purposeful boundaries. But she would have known exactly what to ask for when she went in."

"She must have asked for the ability to control fairies," I said.

My heart was pounding in my chest when I thought of the possibilities. Last winter, the warlock Astravar had managed to turn a good two hundred or so fairies into Cat Sidhe in an attempt to conquer Cimlean City. But he hadn't needed a special gift to do this, and I had a feeling that Lasinta was working on a much larger scale.

"To control a limited number of fairies," Driar Yila said, "she would have needed to know the exact number. So if she knew the exact population of fairies in Faerini, then she could have taken control of them."

"It would work, if she was already working with Ta'lon," Driar Brigel said. "I've seen it in textbooks on fairies that they keep track of their numbers religiously. Each fairy kingdom has very specific and tedious methods of doing this, but it's apparently incredibly accurate."

"Which means this must have been going on an awfully long time," Lonamm said. "Who knows how long the warlocks have been scheming."

"Quite," Driar Brigel said.

My whiskers were twitching as if charged by an electrical storm. I really didn't like what I was hearing; I didn't like it at all. Particularly since a memory had come to me that only I, Seramina, and a few of the White Mages and their unicorns had experienced.

"Lasinta has controlled the fairies before," I said.

If Driar Yila had ears like a cat, they would have shot up at this point. Her gaze snapped onto mine. "What?"

"Back at our school excursion to the Great Barrier," I said. "You know, that time Arran first turned on us. He and Lasinta were still working together, before he turned traitor on her too, and the fairies opened up a portal to the Great Desert in the Fourth Dimension – known in my world as the Sahara – and then Lasinta's magic sent us all tumbling through."

"Another of your secrets that you never told us," Driar Lonamm said accusingly. "When are you going to start communicating with us, Ben?"

I looked over to Esme for support, but she was grooming herself and looking quite entertained by the way I was squirming under Yila's glare. Later I was sure she would corner me and remind me that I'm a cat, and cats never lose staring competitions. So I mustered the courage to stare back.

"I thought the White Mages would have told you," I said. "I can't report everything that I see, or smell, or hear, or taste. There just isn't enough time in the day."

"We don't ask you to report everything, Initiate Ben," Driar Brigel said. "Just the noteworthy things."

"Or maybe you should just learn to ask the right questions, sir, and ma'am, and ma'am."

I imitated a very human bow as I addressed each title, although I'm not sure I did a very good job of this with such a short neck. The Great Driars didn't look very happy with me, but they didn't have time to react.

Because all of a sudden I once again smelled the honey-like scent of a fairy, coming from the double door. The doorway itself disappeared momentarily – tri-coloured crystals and all – and a golden wisp floated through.

Esme and I summoned our staff bearers as it floated down to the ground. Within an instant we had our staffs in our mouths. Warmth rushed to the back of my tongue as I imagined myself using dark magic.

A golden cloud emerged in the centre of the room, and a regal-looking fairy woman stepped out of it. She didn't look happy at all.

19

FAIRY QUEEN

A squeak came from a hole in the wall of the Council Chamber. I spun around to see a tiny nose poking out of a gap in the fireplace stones. Being able to translate the mouse's language, I recognised what it had said.

"Danger, stay away from this one ..."

You'd have thought it was talking about either me or Esme – I don't know which of us it would have found more threatening. But instead it had its gaze fixed on the female fairy who stood before us in human form.

Not many know this, but mice and other creatures that can speak mouse, despite being such social creatures, also like to speak to themselves when alone. Most of this is complaining about the general state of the world. Since I've learned their language, I've heard mice scurrying around saying how there isn't enough food nowadays, and people have to stop locking things in sealed containers. I also heard a mouse once complain that people need to stop putting cheese in mousetraps. It's really not good for their digestive system, apparently.

Now if I were a normal cat, as soon as I'd smelled that

mouse I would have been chasing after it, trying to work out a way to ferret it out. But with this frightening fairy woman in the room, her red cloak whipping behind her, I had a much more pressing issue on my mind.

The fairy in question had shiny, straight red hair that spilled all the way down to her elbows. Her face looked pristine, without a single speck of harshness to be seen on her features. Honestly, she looked like one of those models in the adverts for hair products I used to see on the television back in South Wales.

She smelled of flowers, the way all fairies do – her marked scent being clover and thistle. Her stare had the general spininess of thistle to it as well, and it was directed right at me. The fingers on both her hands twitched.

It would take only one click of her fingers to turn me into whatever she wanted, or to send me anywhere in the Faerie Realm, including thirty feet up in the air. But I also had my staff in my mouth and it would take but one beam to knock her to the floor and paralyse her.

Meanwhile, a dilemma presented itself in my mind. Presumably we had better chances fighting fairy magic with dark magic, but last time I had used dark magic *Cana Dei* had threatened me – and now I was terrified of going anywhere near it.

But then, I hadn't really used very much white magic yet, and I wasn't sure I would be as competent with it as I was with the dark. Therefore I just stood posturing with the staff in my mouth – probably looking ridiculous – as the crystal on Esme's staff started to glow bright white.

"Put down your staffs at once, Initiates," Driar Yila bawled. "This is a diplomatic situation, and we are not in any position to make threats."

"A diplomatic situation?" Esme said. "The fairies are

under the control of the warlocks. We're not negotiating with her but with Lasinta."

I'd never quite worked out how she could speak so eloquently with her staff in her jaws. She'd always said it was done with magic.

The fairy's voice was high-pitched – like fairies' voices often are – but at the same time incredibly commanding. It also clanged as if someone had put thousands of wind chimes in a garden somewhere and set them ringing all at once.

"I've never heard anything so insulting in my entire life," the fairy replied. "Fairies would never ally with warlocks. Throughout history they've been our enemies, but not so much as the dragons whom you've now brought into our realm."

"The warlocks are everyone's enemy, Queen Ca'mun," Driar Brigel said. "They serve no one but themselves and *Cana Dei*. Initiate Ben, Initiate Esme, we're not going to ask you again."

"You'd better do what he says," Queen Ca'mun said, "or I will turn you both into beetles and send you to a field filled with crows."

I looked at Esme and she gave me a blink of approval, though she still waited with her staff in her mouth. Nevertheless I wasn't so sure. Back in the glade, Lasinta had mentioned the fairy queen Ca'mun, saying that she would deal with us. Which meant she probably wasn't our ally.

But then I wasn't going to dare cast any magic after Queen Ca'mun's threat. Crows are vicious enough at my size – I certainly didn't want to contend with them while the size of a beetle.

Once upon a time I'd not thought there to be any worse fate than the tale the two Savannah cats in my neighbourhood had told me about suffocating beneath the belly of a hippopotamus. But since my adventures had started in the First Dimension I'd learned of much, much worse.

I summoned my staff bearer to return my staff to oblivion. Presently Esme did the same.

The fairy queen tossed her head to the side and her hair flowed around her in waves. She'd cast her human glamour to seem as if she had a golden glow about her – to make her look as if she were brimming with power.

She turned her gaze back towards Driar Yila.

"You, Yila, are of royal rank, I believe. So for now you shall represent the humans. As for those who don't know who I am," she glanced at both Esme and me in turn, "I am Queen Ca'mun of the Feyliyane fairy kingdom – the second largest of the four major kingdoms in the Faerie Realm.

"Of course, I've heard they don't teach about the geography of our sacred dimension in human schools, although it is laughable that cats, dogs, dragons, and unicorns should also study within them. But before you say anything, remember that the transportation of dragons into the fairy realm is a breach of the treaty signed between our four kingdoms and your puny principalities of the First Dimension over a thousand years ago."

The fairy queen clicked her fingers. My breath caught in my throat as the air shimmered in front of her. Soon afterwards, a flurry of crimson poppy petals floated to the floor.

Of course the fairy queen wasn't going to kill us with petals, unless she decided to drown us in a sea of the things. Still, her action had made the threat apparent enough – she was in control here and we weren't.

"Queen Ca'mun, with all due respect—" Driar Yila said.

The fairy queen raised her hand and turned her palm towards Yila, her thumb and forefinger delicately poised and ready to click. I watched with guilty satisfaction as a bubble of air travelled down Driar Yila's throat. I'd never in my life seen her so easily cowed.

"Very well, Yila, you may speak," Queen Ca'mun said. "I hope for the sake of your survival that what you say will be worthwhile."

"I just wanted to point out that they are not human schools, but the result of a coordinated cooperation between humans, dragons, and unicorns. The goal of our alliance is a common one – the elimination of the evil cause of the warlocks. We share a common enemy."

The fairy queen let out a mirthful laugh that seemed to shake the very walls of the room. I heard the mouse squeak something inaudible, and the light from the windows was blotted out for a moment. "You have signed treaties of peace with those warlocks, have you not?"

"Not treaties. Temporary truces to give us time to rebuild after we brought an end to the nefarious schemes of the warlock, Astravar."

"And yet, such truces also give your enemy time to rebuild. What is the point of such a paper if you'll just use it to build more weapons of destruction?"

"There are more of us than there are of them, your highness. We have more soldiers and more allies."

"Then why haven't you defeated them yet?"

"Because their magic is great, majesty. They have accumulated between them some of the most powerful crystals in all of the realms."

"Yet you have still not explained to me why you brought yourselves here. Did you want to use the weapons you've amassed to declare war on the fairies too? Because you do not stand a chance against our native magic. We knew the ways of the crystals long before you humans began to lose your fur and learned to strike one stone against another to make fire."

Driar Yila took a deep breath. "If we had the power to

bring ourselves here, suffice to say we would have defeated the warlocks by now. No, our sources tell us that—"

Queen Ca'mun fluttered her palm to shut Driar Yila up. She raised her head and closed her eyes, as if listening for something. The only sound in the room was the faint voice of the mouse moaning about the nature of his existence from deep behind the walls. I really was itching to hunt him down and scoop him out of his hole, but I wisely stayed in place, rooted to the spot.

"Measure your words, Yila," the fairy said after a pause. "Because I hear the crows are particularly hungry this time of year. Low rainfall in the Aisean Wetlands has caused a shortage of beetles."

Fortunately for us all, it seemed that Driar Yila had found her way back to herself. She no longer seemed afraid, or perhaps she had just had enough and was resigned to whatever fate this weird fairy had in store for her.

"I'll put it bluntly," she said. "Lasinta has taken control of the fairies of Faerini. Our sources have revealed that the entire fairy kingdom is under her thrall."

"And how, pray tell me, might that have happened?" Ca'mun asked.

Driar Yila looked down at Esme, as if to imply that she was to blame. It was Esme, after all, who had removed the protective barrier and allowed Lasinta to work her spell.

"Lasinta managed to touch the King's Crystal," Driar Yila said. "She must have stolen a gift ... the ability to control an entire population, perhaps?"

The fairy queen cocked her head, and the glow surrounding her body faded temporarily. She raised her palm once more.

"Give me a moment," she said. "I must commune with my network."

She again clicked her fingers and the magic returned to

her, this time shining even more radiantly than before. Her body lifted up from the ground as she folded her legs underneath her. She closed her eyes.

The walls of the room took on vivid colours, and they wavered as if beginning to melt. All around us the air shimmered in eddying patterns, and the brightness coming off the fairy's skin intensified to such a level that it burned my eyes to look at her.

Even the mouse was now silent. Whiskers, I feared that every single human, and dragon, and cat, and the single dog that resided in this academy would all be turned into beetles to fight for our lives amidst a field of crows. I couldn't even reach out to Salanraja to warn her with the fairy dust blocking our connection.

The fairy opened her eyes, and they glowed so brightly that I couldn't make out her pupils.

"I have need of some of you," she said. "Only a few, mind. And this is non-negotiable."

Presently she clicked her fingers a last time and the room burned with a whiteness that was whiter than any white I'd seen before.

20

AN OLD AND ASHEN FRIEND

The brightness faded, and I found myself lying on the dried leaves of a great forest floor. A waterfall roared nearby, and the air smelled of the freshness of the woods – without so much of the pollen that tends to dominate the Faerie Realm. Rather, this place smelled of crisply fallen leaves and the slightly rocky scent of fresh water.

It made me realise how thirsty I was, and so I started sniffing out the water, my legs following my nose, before I could even see where I was going.

"Careful, Ben," a voice said from behind me. It was softer than Esme's, and it belonged to Seramina. "There's a cliff over there."

Whiskers, the fairy had brought the young teenager here too. But why?

I still had spots before my eyes, and so I felt around my body with my tongue to make sure I still had four and not six appendages – and that I didn't taste of some disgusting beetle. Ca'mun, wherever she was, had not decided to turn me into one.

But for all I knew she could have sent us back to the First

Dimension – somewhere like the Willowed Woods where huge packs of slavering wargs hunted cats like me.

The next voice I heard was not one I wanted to hear.

"Ben, Ben," it barked. It was Max. "We're in the forest, Ben. It's so pretty. Am I dreaming, Ben?"

I blinked, trying to get rid of the bright spots, but they were persistent. Instead, I used my nose to sniff out what was beyond the smelly dog. Esme was somewhere nearby, though I couldn't hear what she was doing. Seramina's snowdrop perfume was also evident, as well as the thick thistly aroma of the fairy queen.

Behind all this was the rich smell of a very ancient kind of tree bark. Somehow I recognised it; in fact I had encountered it not too long ago.

"Ben, I must be dreaming, Ben," Max continued to bark in his rough voice. "Tell me I'm dreaming!"

"I don't think you're dreaming, Max," I said.

"But there's a tree here with a face on it." His voice had now become more of a whine. "And there's a woman floating in front of it. This must be a dream, Ben. When will I wake up?"

Finally the spots in my eyes cleared, and I saw the cliff dropping down in front of me that Seramina had warned me about. At the base of the cliff a waterfall led down to a familiar and spectacular blue lagoon. Where it hit the water, it sent up an impressive spray of white foam. It made me incredibly thirsty just looking at it.

As Max had claimed, Ca'mun was sitting cross-legged, levitating in front of a tree with a massive face etched into its bark. I couldn't see her face, but the face on the tree had its eyes closed.

I also knew who this was, for I'd encountered this tree before. Ca'mun had brought us to talk to one of the most respected 'fairies' in the forest, and I use the word lightly because I've never understood how a gigantic ash tree could be considered a fairy.

Esme was seated beside Seramina, licking her fur and occasionally glancing at the waterfall. Seramina turned to me as she noticed I'd regained full consciousness. She had changed into her white chiffon dress, which provided zero contrast against her pale skin and bright blonde hair. I stalked over to join my friends – safety in numbers and all that.

The Oracle Fairy opened her great barken eyelids just as Ca'mun uncrossed her legs and descended to the floor. The fairy queen turned to face us. Max, on seeing her, scurried over to stand by Seramina. His tail beat against the ground.

"I don't like her! I don't like her! This isn't a dream, it's a nightmare!"

"Max, she's a very dangerous fairy queen and this isn't a dream," Esme snapped back in the dog language. "Now shut up."

Max whimpered and fortunately for all of us he said no more. The fairy queen already had her thumb and forefinger poised as she glared at the dog. Max buried his face in his paws.

Queen Ca'mun took a deep breath.

"This is an honoured occasion for all of you present," she said. "For the Oracle Fairy, also known to some as the Tree of Life or *Yggdrasil*, has requested an audience with the four of you specifically."

"We know who she is," I said. "She's a big ash tree with a very big mouth and the gift to see across time and the dimensions. I even remember her Latin name – *Fraxinus Maximus*, the biggest ash tree of them all."

The fairy queen glared daggers at me, and her upraised hand vibrated with power. But I'd met the Oracle Fairy once before, and I knew that we now had the upper hand here. She wouldn't have summoned us to her glade for this cantankerous fairy queen to destroy us.

In response to my quip, the gigantic ash tree rumbled the surrounding forest with a deep and bellowing laugh. "The crystals might have given you the gift of speaking all languages, Dragoncat, but they didn't grant you the gift of diplomacy."

Esme stalked forwards. "That's what he has a *companion* like me for."

The Oracle Fairy rolled her eyes downwards. "I'm sure he does. As destiny dictated, and as I knew he would. For the last time you and I met, the two of you were at each other's throats."

I looked at Esme. We'd had a lot of quarrels in the past, but really that was just part of being a cat. We also made up quickly – cats unlike humans never like to hold grudges.

"Esme has taught me a lot," I said. "Since we last met, we've saved Bastet from almost dying, and sent the evil Warlock Prince and his pet three-headed Cerberus tumbling into the void."

"I saw, I saw," the Oracle Fairy flexed some of her exposed roots. Their bark rippled and creaked. Several ants scurried out of their tiny home, rushed along the root, and then dived back in again. "You forget that I have grown over the years through the dimensions, and I can see across time and space."

"So we have heard," I said. Her abilities were impressive, admittedly.

The sunken gaze of the tree rolled downwards towards Max. "And last I saw of you, little creature, you'd been literally petrified ... the dog who can walk the dimensions ... It's good to see you looking hale and hearty again."

Max barked in glee and then he started chasing his own tail, as if excitement was hanging off the end of it. "The tree speaks the dog language!" he exclaimed. "The tree speaks the dog language!"

"Ignore him," Esme said. "He gets like that sometimes. Dogs ..."

"Oh, indeed they do. He will uncover his abilities quite soon, you know. And he will become just as powerful as the three of you."

I looked at Max as he continued his goofy dance, and I blinked in disbelief. "You've got to be kidding. Max, an all-powerful mage? He doesn't even know what a warg is."

"You may not believe it now, Dragoncat, but you will see what the future holds. And as for you, Seramina, you have the greatest potential of them all."

Seramina lowered her hands and stared down at her toes. "Everything I've tried has only led to darkness," she said. "If any of us are consumed by *Cana Dei*, we might destroy the worlds."

"That is right," the Oracle Fairy said. "But now Bastet has gifted you with the White Magic to nullify that. What you need now is the confidence to find the balance between the light and the darkness. Only then will you find the strength you need to defeat the warlocks, because that great battle you've envisioned, the one that you saw in the Ghost Realm, is still nigh."

I knew exactly the vision we were talking about – we had gone to the Ghost Realm so I could recover my staff from where Astravar had hidden it. There – where the spirit of everything that has lived, is living, and will live dwells – we'd seen a vision of Seramina fighting the warlocks. She had thrust her staff into the ground and defeated the six remaining warlocks by her own skill alone. But her magic had also splintered the worlds into chunks and summoned all the demons out of the Seventh Dimension to wreak havoc wher-ever they pleased.

"I cannot do it," Seramina said. "I cannot embrace the darkness again."

"But you must," the Oracle Fairy said. "At least not now, but eventually ..."

As the Oracle Fairy spoke, a look of urgency grew on Esme's face. She stepped forward.

"With all due respect, we can discuss philosophy later all you like," she said. "But you summoned us here for a reason, and you specifically summoned the four of us."

"Mind how you speak to the Oracle Fairy," Queen Ca'mun said. "You must practice patience in such things."

Her eyes had once again started to glow a bright white. The air took on that kind of fresh and dangerous smell that happens when molecules start to break apart.

"There is no need to be so threatening to them, Queen Ca'mun," the Oracle Fairy said. "For the Abyssinian is quite right. In my world, time spans across millions of years and it's hard to sometimes focus on the pressing nature of tomorrow. But sometimes I must. Now where was I?"

"About the warlock, Lasinta, I'm guessing," Esme said. "She's taken control of the fairies of Faerini and used them to transport Dragonsbond Academy to the Second Dimension. That much we know."

"Ah yes, ah yes ... now I remember. If the warlocks are successful, they won't only bring Dragonsbond Academy here, but the School of the White where the White Mages are trained, and Bestian Academy where the dragons are trained, and even the Horned Forest where the unicorns are first trained. And if they succeed in that, there will be no stopping them."

"But why?" I asked. "It seems to be a lot of effort to go to for an incredibly elaborate prank."

"It's more than just a prank, Ben," Seramina said with a slow shake of her head. "Bringing the unicorns, dragons and academies here means the threat to the warlocks in the First Dimension is reduced. King Garmin will then have limited resources to guard the crystals in the Versta Caverns, and with no new dragon riders and White Mages to replace the retired guards, over time the warlocks can hunt for whatever crystals they please. That would give them so much power ... immeasurable, consummate power."

Silence ensued. A brief and momentary silence – which wasn't really silence at all, given how loudly the waterfall was crashing below us. A squirrel chittered at us from up in the Oracle Fairy's branches and then scurried off to hide within the thick canopy. Leaves rustled overhead, casting shadows that trembled on the forest floor.

"More than that is at stake, I'm afraid, young Seramina," the Oracle Fairy said momentarily. "And it all has to do with the realm of dreams."

"What do you mean?" I asked.

The Oracle Fairy's lips curled upwards into a thin smile. Across the surface of the great ash tree's bark, whorls started to spin and swirl. "I will show you," she said. "Come into my lake and you will see ..."

There was another rustling of leaves, and steam rose up from the beneath the cliff. It drifted over to us, clearing my sinuses and driving away the headache I'd developed from trying to wrap my head around all this destiny nonsense.

Where the cliff edge met the forest floor, an opening had developed, leading down to the blue lagoon. The waterfall crashed even louder, sending a thin misty spray over the water below.

"Come," the Oracle Fairy said, "and I will show you all you need to see."

CONNECTED DREAMS

A beach of golden fairy dust sloped down gently into the lake, the grains finer than silt. It started from the cliff that the Oracle Fairy – or sacred tree if you must call her that – stood upon and led all the way around to the base of the cascade. The spray from where the waterfall hit the silken blue water rose over the edge of the beach, veiling the edge of it in a thick wet mist.

Honestly, with the force the cascade was hitting the surface of the lake, I would have expected it to have been much more chaotic. But the lake remained as still as a bowl of water – presumably the fairy dust underneath the lake held it in place by magic.

It made me wonder if the whole lagoon and the cliff and the waterfall were all part of one big illusion. For all I knew, this Oracle Fairy – this Tree of Life, this *Yggdrasil* – existed on one flat barren plain, surrounded by glamours. She might not even be a tree, but just a normal fairy like Ta'lon for all I knew.

That was the problem with the Faerie Realm – all these

glamours and this fairy dust made it impossible to tell reality from illusion.

Seramina, Esme, and I stood on the beach at the edge of the water. We'd left the fairy queen, Ca'mun, at the top – apparently it was forbidden for any fairy to enter the Oracle Fairy's sacred lake. Max – like any typical dog – had already jumped in the water and was splashing around. But his efforts didn't generate any waves in the lake – not even ripples. Only his soft panting rolled back out from the water.

"Water's great! Water's great! You have to come in."

He was like the mouse back at Dragonsbond Academy, talking to himself continuously. Except, unlike the mouse, he never seemed to say anything of value. Not many know this, but mice make great philosophers – in fact a mouse might have even inspired a book by a human self-help guru about the existential nature of cheese. Alas, I wish I could say the same about dogs.

I had already tested the water with my foot and found it surprisingly tepid. As a Bengal, a descendant of the great Asian leopard cat, I have always enjoyed a good swim. But Esme eyed the water more tentatively, sitting on settled golden dust far away from where the shore touched the beach.

Seramina also didn't seem to want to go into the water. To make it easier for the girl, Ca'mun had glamoured up a black swimsuit to stretch over Seramina's lithe form in place of her chiffon dress. Though she was a brilliant mage and an excellent academic, she'd never really struck me as much of an athlete.

"This is an insult to cats," Esme said. "Next time I return home to the Fifth Dimension, I'm going to complain to Bastet, I tell you."

"What's the matter?" I asked. "It's only water."

I waded down into the lake to make my point. It tickled at my knees and hocks and sent a comfortable warmth through every muscle in my body. It felt a bit like being healed by White Magic – I could do this all day.

"This is something I've never understood about you, Ben. You've never understood the universal and fundamental law of cats – you don't swim in what you drink."

I took another step into the lake, and the water reached up to my tummy, massaging me gently there. It felt adorable. I also lapped up some of the water with my tongue. After everything that had happened so far, I was incredibly thirsty.

"Here's what the old Ragamuffin back home told me," I answered to Esme. "All cats with able limbs can swim if they are forced to, and then they will swim as well as they stalk."

"Really? Did you ever see him go out for a swim on a Sunday afternoon?"

I tried to imagine it, but all I could picture was the amount of water that that fluffy old cat could have held within his shaggy grey coat.

"He tried swimming once in the fountains of the Alhambra, but then he said it wasn't to his taste."

"Well, it isn't to my taste either. I will enter, but you, Seramina, should go first."

While Esme looked reluctant to enter the water, Seramina looked absolutely terrified of it. "I've never swam in my life before," she said.

"Then now is a good time to start," Esme snapped back.

"But ... wait, it said in my book that Abyssinians quite like the water. Just like Bengals, you should take to it quite naturally."

"Not this Abyssinian," Esme said, and she turned her body to the side so she was parallel to the shore. "Look, I've spent most of my life in training with Bastet on her island on the River of Souls. That river is fatal for any creature that falls in. So, if you don't mind, I'd rather you went ahead first."

"But I already told you," Seramina said. "I can't swim …"

See, what did I tell you? Other than riding dragons, Seramina seemed to abhor any sort of activity. You'd sooner find her nose in a book than chasing the next runner to the end of the track.

I went further into the water until I was floating. The lake closed in to surround me in its embrace. It not only soothed me, but I also started to see images in my mind that I had never seen before. An orange dinosaur teddy bear on pink silk sheets. A golden fairy wisp changing into an athletic female human to do a somersault in mid-air, then changing back again before she hit the ground. A cloud that turned into a bear, then a fairy, and then the long form of a serpent.

I smelled all kinds of rich scents, most of them pleasant. Jasmine and honey and crushed catnip and smoky mutton sausages. All of them melded together into a rich cocktail that pulled me further in.

I knew these sensations weren't from the Faerie Realm, nor did they belong to my own mind. Rather, it felt as though I was peering into other minds – a vast tapestry of conscious-ness, so different from my own. As the images came, the lake beneath me took on a soft glow. But this soon faded, and the visions withered away.

The Oracle Fairy's voice boomed down from the part of the cliff face that didn't have water falling from it. "I thought you'd be ready by now," she said. "You are certainly taking your time down there. Didn't you say we didn't have much of it?"

This wasn't much help really, coming from an ancient being who could see across time and space. I realised Seramina was going to need some encouragement to get in the water and Esme's reluctance wasn't much help here.

"Look, swimming's easy," I said to Seramina. "You just lie on the water and kick your legs like this."

"But what if I sink?" she called back.

In all the time I'd known Seramina, I'd never known her to be so much of a wimp about something so trivial.

"You won't sink. Look, all humans need to do is move their arms and legs in circles. I'd show you, but my joints won't allow it."

Seramina shook her head. "I wish Asinda were here to help. Or Ange ... or even Rine."

"Just get in and I'll show you. Esme, help her out, will you?"

"I've got a better idea," Esme said, and her staff bearer winked out of oblivion just in front of her. As her staff bearer lunged down towards her with her staff, she dashed forward and stopped right next to Seramina.

Next thing I knew, her staff was in her mouth and the crystal on it was glowing white. Esme always seemed to use White Magic. I'd never, ever seen her cast dark, though I knew she had the ability.

"Esme, you can't cast magic," I said as quickly as I could. "That queen Ca'mun will turn us into beetles and—"

But either she didn't want to listen, or I couldn't get the words out fast enough, because a bright white light quickly enveloped Seramina and the Abyssinian, concealing them from view. The light faded to display a bubble, buoying the girl and cat above the ground.

To the untrained eye, the bubble might have seemed to move of its own accord, but within its walls I could see Esme focused on guiding it. It drifted over to where Max and I were swimming, basking in the wonderfully warm waters. It stopped between us, its base just barely touching the lake surface.

"There," Esme said. Her voice came out muffled but still

found its way through the bubble's thin wall. "We've done what the Oracle Fairy asked."

"Too right you have," I said. "Although you're not technically *in* the lake."

I glanced up at the cliff edge and saw Queen Ca'mun standing there, observing with her hands on her hips. She didn't look happy with Esme's antics, and my gut feeling told me that if I didn't do something to get both females in the water then she would.

Without thinking, I paddled over to the bubble and swiped at it with my sharp extended claws.

Pop!

They fell, and plopped into the water. They made such a huge splash that it sprayed out all over Max and me. Still, there were no ripples and the water settled instantaneously.

As I had predicted, Esme found her footing quite fast, though as she had fallen her staff had dropped into the water, and she clumsily tried to paddle towards it.

Meanwhile, Seramina floundered about in the water, hyperventilating and flailing her arms and legs in every possible direction. For a moment I thought I had made a bad decision.

"What did you do, Ben?" Max barked. "That was mean!"

But his barking wasn't going to help the situation. Instead, I swam over to Seramina, and I looked at her right in the eye. As her arms and legs whipped about, her face was red and her eyes were wide with panic.

"I can't swim, Ben," she said. "I can't swim, and none of you are strong enough to hold me up."

"Just relax," I said. "Seramina, you can handle this."

I felt bad – I felt really bad. I shouldn't have forced her into the water.

Her head went under for a moment, and those few

seconds seemed to last for minutes. Then she emerged, sputtering water.

"Ben, I ... Just help!"

She went under again, and I got ready to dive under to at least push her back up again. But Max was faster; he dived in front of me, right underneath the water. With a remarkable feat of agility, he somehow managed to tuck his nose underneath Seramina's arms, and then push her back to the surface again.

"Hold on," he whined in the dog language. "I can hold you. I must hold you."

Seramina was safe for now, but I felt absolutely terrible. A monster. And I had only intended it as a prank ...

The voice of the Oracle Fairy boomed down from the cliff face.

"I see I'm a little slow to react. I apologise; I'm getting a little lethargic in my old age. For immortals of nature and the earth like me, things happen in cycles, you see."

Her voice was so loud that it generated a temporary disturbance in the water. Despite that, the pool clearly favoured stillness, and so the waves only whipped out over the lake and then immediately settled, as if they hadn't been there at all.

Seramina had calmed now, staring ahead of her with red eyes, Max buoying her upwards. Esme had managed to retrieve her staff from the water and her staff bearer had plucked it into oblivion. Strangely, she seemed to be enjoying the swim, paddling about almost as eagerly as Max had been.

"Now, where was I?" the Oracle Fairy continued. "Oh yes, the water ... now close your eyes, it's time to dream. And don't worry, Seramina, I'll make sure that you stay afloat."

Once again the lagoon took on that glow, getting visibly brighter. I saw even stranger visions – a tiny dragon riding a massive unicorn; a shark leaping out of the ocean over a yacht and then sailing further over the moon; a twenty-foot, beautiful woman with blonde flowing hair and glowing skin, wearing a pale silken dress and with a kind, soft gaze.

The water was warm. Everything felt so comfortable.

I closed my eyes and, though I remained awake, I fell into a deep and vivid dream.

MEET THE GODDESS

I t didn't take long for me to see again, but I was not in the Faerie Realm.

The same woman I'd encountered in the incredibly brief vision – the glowing giant beautiful woman – stood before us. I walked up to her so I could at least sniff her feet, which didn't smell like feet at all. Rather, they smelled fresh, like an abundant waterfall, like a clearing storm, like the moment the smell of grass is washed away by dew.

We had left the water, and now stood at her feet on an island of the same fine and shining sand as we'd seen in the Faerie Realm. A cratered mountain rose behind the giant woman, green at its bottom and dark at its top. It disappeared into a thin layer of fluffy clouds, above which spanned a rich and vivid sky limned with the shades of amber that come just after sunset.

Everything here seemed so soft – the light, the texture of the swishing sea that licked the sand, and the gaze of this woman, despite her enormous size.

Esme, Seramina, Max, and I had all been brought here. I could have sworn it was just a dream, but somehow it felt as if we were sharing the same dream together. Was that even possible? I did know that when I'd first met Seramina, she had somehow visited my dreams.

My friends seemed to still be adjusting to our new environment, so I decided to address the woman first.

"Who the whiskers are you?" I asked.

She lowered her head slowly, and her gaze followed it. Every single movement of hers seemed to be so gentle. This woman hadn't been born to frighten.

"You have met other immortals throughout the realms, I believe," she said.

Like my crystal, she spoke in a gently lilting Welsh accent. Except her voice was much smoother, and it not only seemed to come out of her lips but also to roll off the water. Esme came up to sit next to me. She looked up at the woman and I detected a whiff of fear from her.

"Be careful what you say, Ben. Because not all immortals are as kind as they appear ..."

I looked at Esme, admittedly a little startled. I mean, we cats have something in our genes that tells us whom to trust and whom not to trust when we first meet them. Still, patience isn't carved into our genetic makeup, and I really hate it when someone doesn't get right to the point.

"So, who are you exactly?" I asked.

"She's beautiful," Max panted. "She's beautiful. Can she be my new master?"

"Shut up, Max," I barked in the dog language, and then I jumped as Esme barked it at the same time.

I often forgot that Max didn't speak the human language. But if this giant woman was anything like Bastet, then she'd be able to speak all our languages at once.

"Look, great giant woman person with shiny skin," I said. "We have a world to save, and all you immortals seem to be so slow to get anything done. So I ask again, with as much patience as I can muster right now, who are you?"

The woman's lips curled upwards into a gentle smile. "My name is Brigit," she said. "I am a muse to many, and I live here in this world, guarding dreamers from the nightmares which might destroy them and smoothing their transition back to the waking world."

"Whiskers, please don't tell me there's a ninth dimension – because I've already found eight of them hard enough to comprehend."

"That depends on what you mean by dimension, because you can be in this place and in any of the other dimensions at the same time."

She paused a moment, as if knowing the concept might take a while to sink in.

In all honesty, the gift of being able to speak multiple languages had left me confused regarding what exactly a dimension was. In many human languages of the Fourth Dimension, there were in fact only four 'dimensions' formed by three units of distance and one of time.

Some scientists in the Fourth Dimension believed in more dimensions, but that had something to do with pieces of string. I cannot wrap my head around all these nonsense theories in their language, known as 'modern physics'. String is only interesting when curled up in a ball. It loses its appeal once fully unravelled and strewn out across the room. The same can be said about space-time, I guess, which completely proves my point. Dimensionality is a funny and confusing thing.

Meanwhile, the humans in the First Dimension have introduced me to Dimensions with a capital 'D', linked together through portals and other devices. These dimensions are also completely different from each other. The hardest one to understand is the Sixth Dimension, that bridges the other dimensions and allows to you to flit between them as if they were channels on the television.

"Brigit," Esme said, interrupting my daydreams, "Bastet knows you. She told me she communes with you sometimes."

"Of course she does," Brigit said. "For even gods and goddesses must dream."

"Wait," Seramina said. "I've read about you in books. I thought you were the goddess of fire and poetry."

"And livestock, and healing, and agriculture," Esme said.

"I am of those, among many other things," the goddess said. "Because where truly does inspiration lie? But for now, I am to be your guide within the dream world. For the Oracle Fairy has requested that you should be taken through a *woken* dream ... This is the only one way to traverse the dreams of others. You are privileged indeed."

She swept out her arm, and curled out her finger towards the other side of beach. Before where there had been only sky and palm trees, there was now a doorway standing there, haloed with white light just as a portal would be. It had on it four panelled windows and the number seven etched onto its surface. Rainbows shimmered in the reflections on the windows. The patterns in the woodwork seemed to swirl softly, and the door smelled of fresh wood and sawdust, as if it had just been delivered by the carpenter.

"I know that door ..." Seramina said. Her voice was strained. "The portal to the world of *woken* dreams. No ... after Astravar and Arran, I said I would never dreamwalk again."

"Dreamwalking?" I asked. Come to think of it, Seramina had first been introduced to me as a 'dreamwalker'.

"You can die while dreamwalking," she explained. "If your body is asleep and you die in your own dream, then you wake up – it's how dreams are broken. But if your body is awake, and you die in someone else's dream ..."

"Indeed, there would be no return for you," Brigit said. A soothing, crisp and leafy scent floated over from her. It was as if she could sense my fear and had her own way of easing it.

"Wait," I said. "Could someone please just tell me what is going on here? We have met fairies, and warlocks, and a talking tree, and now you are teleporting us from place to place and telling us that we must do things, but no one is telling us why."

Brigit took in a breath. It wasn't a heavy breath, but a slow and careful one. She turned towards the sea. Out of it drifted the scent of salt and seashells.

"Would you care to explain what you know, *Yggdrasil?*"

"Certainly," came the deep, resonant voice of the Oracle Fairy. Above the sea, the air shimmered, and the tree with the face in it appeared in her full glory. "I guess I have left some matters absent in their minds."

"What are you doing here?" I asked.

"As I have already told you – my roots span across space and time, and also they plunge into the very fabric of dreams."

"Then, given you're in the know, how does our mysterious quest have anything to do with dreams?" I asked.

"Well," said the Oracle Fairy. "What do you think fairies think of all day? Why do you think fairies and humans find it so hard to understand each other?"

"Wait ... don't tell me. You're going to say they're dreamers, aren't you?"

The tree wrinkled up her nose and seemed to sniff at the air. I wondered if she herself were dreaming.

"It's not the fairies themselves," she said. "It's the fairy dust. The very nature of it connects the fairies' minds together, and anyone who visits this realm. That's how fairy magic works, it connects one mind to another through *woken* dreams. That's also what makes fairy magic so dangerous;

sometimes, misused dust can drive a creature irrecoverably insane."

"And so how does Lasinta fit into all this?" Seramina asked. "What is she up to?"

"It's not the first time someone has tried to take dominion over the fairy realm, and the dreams they connect to. Once, the warlock Astravar used this ability to try to use an army of Cat Sidhe to overcome Cimlean City."

"I know," I said. "We were the ones who stopped him."

"Ah yes," the Oracle Fairy said. "When time is so deep, sometimes one forgets the granularity of such events. But Lasinta's plan is different, and in fact we don't understand its true nature. All we know is that she wants to manipulate the world of dreams and is using the fairies to do so. But for what purpose, none of us have any idea."

"Wait," I said. "I thought that you could read the future and that your roots extended throughout all possibilities in time and space."

The Oracle Fairy paused. If a tree could breathe, I might imagine her taking a deep breath at this point. Instead, her gaze shifted over to Brigit. In this dream, a pink glow seemed to shimmer over her bark. I could smell not only the salt and the sea, but the essence of a kind of magic drifting off the water as though from a distant island. It wasn't dark magic, but something pure and noble – a little redolent of acorns, I guess.

"No one can predict the nature of dreams," Brigit said. "There is no destiny or foretelling in this realm, because the dream world has a life of its own. While the eight dimensions are determined by the rules of cause and effect, anything can happen in a dream. Sometimes dreams will connect to the essence of reality and read the forecasts of the crystals in the real world, but nobody knows how they do it – neither the gods and goddesses, nor any other immortals, let alone the crystals themselves. But I can tell you that dreams and reality can sometimes intersect in profound ways ... unexpected ways."

"You mean to say you govern a realm you don't truly understand?" I asked. "How is that even possible?"

"Everything is possible in the realm of dreams," Brigit said. "Expand your mind, young Dragoncat, and you will eventually see that. Although in many cases it can take hundreds of years."

My ears perked up as I heard the distant screech of what must have been a thousand swallows from the distant island. Then came an orchestra of nightingales, the coos of cuckoos, and the grunts of a satisfied boar after a good meal of berries. I turned my head slightly to the side, to see that the tree had disappeared. Now there was only a distant yacht, glowing whitecaps, and seagulls circling above the water looking for fish.

Esme took a step nearer to the door. I also moved towards it.

"I guess you're telling us that you want us to go in and investigate what Lasinta is up to?" Esme asked. "And if I'm right in understanding, if we die in the dream then we won't wake up?"

"Bastet always did say you were a fast learner, Esme of the White," Brigit said. "Perhaps the most diligent student in all of Dragonsbond Academy. Though you, Seramina, and the leaf mage Ange might make close contenders."

"So, another adventure," Seramina said, seeming unfazed by the compliment, and a long sigh ensued. "This time in a random world, and more darkness to pursue. Great ..."

"I understand," Max barked. "I understand you all. The wind translates for me! I can understand the cat language. You can't keep secrets from me anymore."

I growled at him. Meanwhile, Esme took a few more steps

towards the doorway, and then I leapt forwards and overtook her. I looked back over my shoulder.

"Well, what are we waiting for?" I said. "Come on, slow-coaches."

It might not have been the real world, but I had a feeling that in the dream world I could eat whatever food I wanted. My tummy was rumbling, and I didn't know if it was my real stomach or my dream one. But at that moment I didn't care.

I might find smoked salmon, which I'd only had once since I'd left the Fourth Dimension, and I really, really missed it. Or I might find some foods I'd never tried before. The old Ragamuffin had once told me that caviar is surprisingly tasty ... he remembered it from when he was a kitten back in Spain. Fish eggs, who'd have thought?

"Just one more thing—" Brigit called after me. "You have three Guardians of the White among you, and one yet to be. Yet still you are missing a key member. Convince her to join you."

"Asinda ..." Esme said. "But where will we find her?"

"In the dream world, it isn't a question of 'where'. Make the connections, and you will find your way. The rules of a *woken* dream are much different to those of a regular one. You cannot be told them, you will have to discover them as you go along."

"But do you want us to bring Asinda into the dream world or the Faerie Realm?" Seramina asked. Her silver hair also had a pink sheen to it. It made her look slightly like a hippy.

"Bring her wherever you must. Only know that the Oracle Fairy will open a portal for her at the Tower of the Grand. She must climb to the top of it to enter the portal."

I took note of that detail. I thought it might be important later.

"If the Oracle Fairy is going to open a portal for her,"

Seramina said, "I presume it will take her to the Faerie Realm. She can't open a portal into the world of dreams, can he?"

Brigit didn't answer, but she didn't need to, because Esme filled in the gap for her. "We might need Asinda in the Faerie Realm if we are to go up against Lasinta there."

I rubbed my nose against hers. It was drier than usual. "You're so wise, Esme."

"I know," she replied.

The door opened in front of us, and a light streamed out of it. I would like to say it was a white light, but in all honesty I couldn't tell its colour. As soon as my mind attached a colour to it, it changed to another one.

Or perhaps it was all colours at once. It could have been white, or it could have been brown. But then, is there such a thing as brown light? I'm not sure I've ever seen it.

"Everyone has the same thoughts about the nature of light that you're having," Brigit said. "But it really doesn't matter. Now go."

We didn't wait a moment – not even Seramina. Because the dream world awaited us on the other side and – in spite of the danger – so did the answers which we were all deeply longing for.

23

DREAM CRASHING

The light only led to more light, which led to a twisting and turning dizziness. I sprinted through the brightness, unable to see any of my friends around me. But after a while I realised that I wasn't even running on solid ground.

There was a high-pitched noise coming from somewhere that sounded a bit like a faulty live wire. The lights formed spots before my eyes, but then as I stopped to look around, I could see my friends very faintly.

Only Max continued to run, which was rather comical as he seemed to be on a suspended treadmill. Esme and Seramina instead were lying down on thin air, floating as we rotated in a broad circle. To the sides, I could see rings arranged to form a twisting tunnel that led into the sea, from where I'd heard the sound of wildlife before.

Some mysterious force was pushing it through the tunnel at high speed, and this tunnel kept diving and twisting and looping around itself. I tried to focus on the water but then I felt sick every time it looked as if we'd plunge into the furiously churning sea. It didn't look as forgiving up close as it had from the island.

For a while I thought I might throw up. Whiskers, I'd thought seasickness was bad.

I closed my eyes and waited for it all to be over. This tunnel felt worse than flying on Salanraja when she was in one of her bad moods. My body seemed to be telling me that I would die in this tunnel.

I don't know for how long I kept telling myself that, or what happened when I eventually left the tunnel.

I just know that enough time had passed ...

"Bengie, there you are," Salanraja said in my mind. *"I was wondering what might have happened to you. I felt so drowsy all of a sudden, and then—"*

"Salanraja," I said, cutting her off. *"Is that really you?"*

"Of course it's me, Bengie ..."

"Ben," I said.

"Bengie ... this is my dream and I can dare to call you whatever I want."

I ventured to open my eyes. Indeed, I was on Salanraja's back, nestled within her corridor of spikes. We were flying over the vast sea that the tunnel had rolled us over, except now the tunnel was nowhere to be seen.

I looked down over Salanraja's back, looking for fish in the water. Salmon perhaps, or maybe whales or dolphins. I couldn't see any life, only a threatening tumult. The waves crashed and roared vociferously and upon the air I could taste the humidity of an approaching storm.

We were so high up that if Salanraja decided to throw me into it then I'd surely perish. Who knew what she'd decide to do in her own dream.

"Salanraja, we need to find land," I said. *"There's a thunderstorm approaching."*

"Gracious demons, don't be silly Bengie ... there's no clouds. Look at that bright shining sun ..."

Indeed, I could feel its heat beating down upon my back.

It made me want to lie down and go to sleep, but I was already asleep, asleep in Salanraja's dream ... And yet at the same time awake. Whiskers, this was all so confusing.

"*Salanraja, you have to listen to—*"

"*Please, Ben, you're so anxious all the time. Always so jittery, and I have to listen to your thoughts roiling inside your mind like thunderstorms. This is my dream now, and I demand you give me time to relax.*"

"*You don't understand, Salanraja ... I can't die here.*"

"*What do you mean you can't die? This is a dream. You die or I die, and then I wake up. That's how it's always worked.*"

"*You don't understand. This is no normal dream, this is —*" what was that term Brigit had used again? I racked my brain to remember. Ah yes ... "*—Salanraja, this is a* woken *dream.*"

"*A what?*"

"*A* woken *dream. Salanraja, if I die here, I die forever.*"

"*Yada yada yada. Always so jittery, Bengie.*"

"*Salanraja, I'm—*"

"*Hang on Bengie, extreme dive ... I hope you like to swim.*"

She plunged down so fast that it was like a scaly floor had fallen from beneath me. The wind whipped against my face so hard that I couldn't breathe. I couldn't hear myself think.

Salanraja was diving faster than a body could fall. The water lunged up towards us.

"*Salanraja, this is too fast!*"

Too late ...

There came a crash of thunder, and everything went black.

24

DREAM BATTLE

I returned to the pathways, twisting and turning through time and space. The rings of light that formed the passageway revolved around their centres as I passed through them. Beneath me the ocean churned, and soon I realised it wasn't an ocean at all but an impression of many different landscapes. I drifted from one to the other, as the medium that transported me tried to take me to another dream. My head spun, and I wanted out of this thing, back to Aleam's workshop with a bowl of mackerel in front of me. Immortals kept sending me on harrowing quests, and all I'd ever wanted was a good meal.

All of a sudden there was blackness, and I felt myself falling through worlds, millions of them, linked together by one finely woven and elaborate thread—

I hit the ground, and everything spun, and there came another flash of light ...

"Manipulator!"

The cry had come from Rine, somewhere nearby.

I spat dust out of my mouth, coughing. All I could see was bright light. Was I dead? Or was it just another dream?

No, I'd been lucky. Salanraja had woken up just before we'd crashed into the turbulent sea. Brigit after all had told us that she protected dreamers from nightmares—

"Ben, watch out!" Ange shouted.

The urgency in her voice sent my muscles into action. I dived wherever my limbs would take me. The pain of movement ached even worse than the agony of transforming into a chimera.

Next to me the ground sizzled. I felt an intense heat, and debris scratched against my flank. Then came the mixed stench of charred earth and rotten vegetable juice.

"I've got it," Rine said. "Hang on."

Within the white light, a blue beam streaked out in front of me. Something popped, then crackled. The air smelled like ozone.

The light faded and I saw a lifeless grey crystal tumble to the ground. A terrifying screech came from the sky, a sound far more eldritch than what any living vocal cords could make.

I craned my head to see the spindly form of a bone dragon cutting across the purple sky. It seemed to cut a blood red crescent moon in half and then swooped around and back towards us.

I called for my staff bearer but it didn't come. Whiskers, I couldn't even summon my staff bearer. But then this wasn't my dream.

Instead I stood frozen to the spot, the hackles on my back so sharp that they seemed to want to tear my skin. Even my face felt frozen as I watched the terrifying skull of that bone dragon diving, it's mouth wide open on its single bone hinge. Those sharp teeth could rip me to shreds, and a purple acidic cloud would soon come out from its magical centre deep within.

Suddenly, a vine whipped across the landscape, followed

by a trailing glowing wisp. It lashed out at the bone dragon's neck, and its head crashed to the ground just short of the whiskers on my paws.

The bone dragon's body came down after the head, and it contained enough solid bone to crush me under its velocity and weight. Instead it crumbled into ash as it rolled forward, covering me in a blanket of smelly dust.

I sneezed, then I shook as much of the stuff off me as I could. I hated it when stuff like that got into my fur. I'd need a good grooming now, which meant I'd have to taste the stuff as well. I couldn't think of anything worse at that moment than eating the charred remains of a bone dragon. It would pollute my blood for eternity.

Rine plunged his staff into the ground and then tossed his head back and guffawed. We were in the land that I always dreaded to enter – a barren wasteland of flat, grey, lifeless cracked rock fringed by smelly purple clouds.

We all know what those clouds smelled like – rotten vegetable juice. Which meant dark magic pervaded the landscape here and I could be nowhere else but the Darklands – the chosen home of the warlocks.

"Ben, why haven't you got your staff?" Rine called. "There's more of them coming."

Really, I would have thought the land was entirely bare. But I only needed to blink and dozens of them were suddenly there, strewn out across the dry earth. Wispy shimmering forms which took on a vaguely humanoid shape and had their spectral staffs ready for battle – ready to destroy us all.

More screeches came down from the grey and purple sky. There must be thousands of bone dragons up there.

"*Salanraja, are you there?*" I asked in my mind.

No response.

So I'd left her dream – she'd probably woken up.

Whose dream was this, then? Rine's or Ange's?

A manipulator turned towards me and shot out a white beam. I darted out of the way just in time, tumbling over the ground. As I recovered from my roll, the giant hand that was my staff bearer plunged down from the sky and placed my staff in my mouth.

Except it didn't feel right; it was limp, and tasted of grass, and had a single poppy dangling from its end where the crystal should have been. The crimson flower looked like it was about to fall off its stalk.

Whiskers, if I died in this dream, I would die forever ... in short, I was doomed.

Another manipulator was towering over me. It angled its glowing head downwards and pointed its staff at me. Manipulators have no face, but still in its poise I could read its intent. It wanted to end me.

"Hang on, Ben," Ange said. "Help is coming."

All of a sudden there came a sound of rushing air and the stench of foetid breath. Out from behind me came a thunder of paws and a desert cheetah plunged out of nothing at full speed.

Ange's pet, Palimali, charged forward, straight at the manipulator that was about to crush me under its staff. She took its crystal heart in her mouth and the manipulator vanished in a brief flash like that of a camera.

Palimali continued her momentum through a row of manipulators standing before me. She passed through their ethereal bodies and spat out crystals faster than I'd ever seen her sprint. She must have been moving at a thousand miles an hour, because it was over in less than a second.

"We did it!" Rine shouted. "Well done, Ange ... you and your cheetah, we beat them all!"

He patted her on the back. But Ange didn't look pleased; in fact, I could smell her fear. In this dream, her heart was beating so loudly it sounded like an imp playing the bongos within her chest. Her lips trembled as her eyes stared right up at something in the sky.

One moment there were only clouds, then there was a giant looming over us all. He had a purple bobbled cloak and a grey face with fissures in that made it look like a cracked eggshell. He had terrible burning eyes and no hair. I knew him, for I'd defeated him long ago.

Astravar...

He shifted his gaze down towards me. "There you are, Dragoncat. I've been looking for you all this time, and now beyond the grave I have my chance to destroy you."

"Don't worry, Ange," Rine said. "I'll deal with him."

An icicle shot out from the glowing blue crystal on his staff. It spun right towards Astravar's giant heart, gaining in size and momentum. But Astravar lifted his hand, and Rine's magic hovered there just in front of the warlock.

"Fool!" Astravar shouted, snapping his head towards Rine.

He turned his giant staff towards the young man, and a red beam shot out of his purple crystal. It hit him on the chest and sent him into oblivion in a puff of smoke. The magic didn't even make a smell.

"*No!*" Ange screamed. Her jaw tightened. "You are meant to be dead!"

"Well, clearly I am not."

"No matter ... I will make you pay."

I recognised the wicked and cruel laugh that came from Astravar's mouth as it pealed out over the rocks. It was laced with madness and for the few moments it lasted, it seemed as if it would never end.

Astravar pointed his staff at Ange, and his face twisted. He didn't even need to cast a beam of magic at her – the vines twisted their way up around Ange's body, entangling her within her own school of magic.

"All this study; all this hard work," Astravar said. "And you never grew strong enough to defeat a warlock, young Ange. You will never be as strong as someone like Seramina. It's just not in your blood."

The same vines twisted around me. They found their way around my legs, my face, my chest. They tightened until I reached the point where I could hardly breathe.

I tried to wriggle free, to summon magic out of the flower dangling from my staff, anything ... but this was clearly Ange's dream, and so I had no power here. To my side, I could hear her muffled voice through a gag of vines.

"Now, it is time for me to end Dragoncat's life," Astravar said, his eyes now narrow slits, "because I've always wanted revenge for what he's done. Meanwhile all you can do is watch, Initiate Ange. You have always been hopeless like that. Always second best ..."

A second red beam shot out of Astravar's staff. It hit me right at the front of the chest. A sharp stabbing pain wracked my muscles and the stench of burning fur flooded my nostrils.

"No!" Ange shouted. "You'll kill him! Stop it, Astravar – stop it!"

Suddenly, everything went black.

25

FAILED CURE

Again, the tunnel. Spinning through it; light flashing everywhere; being yanked from edge to edge; my head thumping. Still that burning sensation throbbing in my chest.

How many dreams would I have to go through?

How many times would I have to die?

Or perhaps I was dead already, tumbling through the void, never able to find equilibrium. Was this how it was all meant to end?

I landed on a cold stone floor, tumbling over the cobbles. I picked myself up, finding purchase in the pores of the stones with my claws. I still couldn't see – bright white light was everywhere. But this place had a familiar smell – of cat, and mackerel, and all the chemicals necessary for alchemy and healing.

I saw spots, but then they faded and I looked up to see Aleam peering over at me – hunched over his staff. The crystal on it was yellow and smelled slightly of amber. He looked more pallid than when I last remembered seeing him. His eyes had sunken into their sockets, and his skin seemed to hang off his jowls.

"Ben," he said. He leaned down and stroked me under the chin. I found myself purring, glad not to have landed in another ordeal. "Glad you're finally out of there …"

He didn't smell right, and I couldn't put a claw on why. But there was something deathly seeping out of the pores of his skin.

"Out of where?" I asked. "Wait, Aleam, do you know what's going on?"

"Well of course, I had to rescue you from a field of mandragoras, remember? You took their poison, and really, I thought you were going to die."

There came a banging at the door which startled me. I scurried into a corner. A gruff male voice came from behind the door.

"Driar Aleam," the voice said. "Open the door now or we will have to take it by force."

Aleam looked down at me and chuckled. He sounded nervous. "I'm going to have to take that, Ben. Just give me a minute."

He hobbled towards the door, his step not having that normal spring to it. The hinges let out a stiff creak as it opened. A bald man in a white robe, sitting on top of a unicorn, waited at the door. The unicorn's horn glowed white, as if ready to cast magic. The man had a long scroll held in front of him. From it he began to read.

"Yes, let's see here … ahem. Driar Aleam, you are hereby under arrest by order of the king for your unsanctioned use of dark magic. You must come with the White Guard at once. Any attempt to resist may result in your immediate termination."

Whiskers, this wasn't good … but then it was a dream. Nothing could happen to Aleam, surely.

But I didn't feel good, either. I had the sensation of the

pores in my skin opening up, letting anything beneath them ooze out, my follicles stretching and pinching the tissue in between. I looked down on the ground to see my fur lying there in great clumps. It had lost its colour, the brilliant orange suffusing to a dull grey. My head was spinning. And that stench of death – it hadn't been coming from Aleam.

It was coming from within me. The stench of my own demise.

Aleam looked back at me. "Ben, are you okay? Fiery demons, I didn't give you enough of the antidote." He turned back to man in the doorway. "Hang on a moment, please. I'll be right with you."

"Driar Aleam, as the edict states, any attempt to resist arrest will result in your own termination."

Steam rose from an open tube in Driar Aleam's alembic, on his worktable. From an open spout, I could see a yellow liquid dripping onto the floor. Forming a puddle. If I could only reach it.

Yet I felt so weak. My muscles could not move. Everything in my body shook, and I collapsed to the floor, groaning. I could feel the burning in the place where the mandragora – that horrible plant with its snapping jaws like a gigantic and agile Venus flytrap – had bitten me on the flank.

"Ben ... please. I just need to help him."

"I'm sorry, Driar Aleam, these orders have come directly from the king."

"I just ... I must do this."

Driar Aleam stepped away from the door towards his apparatus. At the same time, a wide white beam came out of the unicorn's horn and hit Aleam on the back of the shoulder. I felt the searing heat, and Aleam's body froze as a paralysing white shield wrapped around him.

I wanted to go over to help him, to turn into a chimera

perhaps and teach that smelly unicorn a lesson. But I was so helpless. I couldn't move ...

The last thing I saw was the expression on Aleam's face. It was one of guilt – of believing he had failed me.

Thus, in another dream, I died.

Once again everything faded to black.

26

A CHANCE FOR REBIRTH

This time, I didn't awaken to bright white light, nor did I find myself yanked about by the mystical tunnel that threaded the pathways between dreams.

Rather I saw only blackness, so deep that my eyes started to see random shapes within it. Here there was no sensation of hot and cold, nothing to touch, and a scent I knew well. This time, it wasn't rotten vegetable juice but something more akin to yeast extract. The scent of the Ghost Realm, aka the Third Dimension – the final place where souls end up reliving every moment of their past.

Whiskers, I had died, hadn't I? Aleam's dream had been the one that ended me.

Out of all possible ironies, the famous Dragoncat, descendant of the great Asian leopard cat and the mighty George, vanquisher of warlocks, hadn't been finished in action. Rather I'd died in one of Aleam's dreams based on the memory of a cure he had given me a long time ago. And in his dream his methods had gone awry.

Why was everyone dreaming of me dying, anyway? What was wrong with these people?

I lifted myself on all fours and started to walk in whatever direction I could. I couldn't see anything – not even my own body – but I'd been to the Ghost Realm before, and so I knew that if I wondered for long enough, I'd encounter visions of my past. Or, if I was lucky, I might even meet some of my ancestors.

Some of them might not be so friendly, admittedly. The last time I'd entered this place, some great Asian leopard cats had almost torn me to shreds. But right now I would take on anything to ward off the darkness. I would even visit the fiery peaks of the Seventh Dimension if I had to.

"Be careful what you wish for, Dragoncat."

The voice came out of the darkness, resonant and smooth, in a language so ancient that I don't think I'd heard it spoken before. It had a deep timbre to it, but not so much that I could determine its gender. Still, it had a kind of enticing power in it that made me want to submit to its will.

"Who are you?" I said in that same ancient language. "Reveal yourself."

"Certainly ... although you must always remember that there are some things you cannot see."

"I said reveal yourself!"

"Very well."

There came a flash of white, as if lightning had just streaked through the darkness. Then I saw that same darkness, pulsing in front of me in a great spherical orb.

I wouldn't have been able to see it had it not been for the dancing, white, glowing specks that leapt out of its surface and then disappeared back into it again. They looked like minnows that had for whatever reason decided to leap out of a vast ocean, because they didn't want to exist in this all-encompassing void.

My heart pounded, and my breath caught at the back of my throat. I knew exactly what I was looking at, for I had seen its inverse as a ball of White Magic – the magic that creates by absorbing destruction.

But now I was looking at the darkness that absorbs creation.

I was staring right into the heart of *Cana Dei*.

"So I'm dead," I said, "and here you find me in the Ghost Realm. Maybe I can finally use my retirement to defeat you."

"You could as much defeat me as you could defeat the wind, Dragoncat. Why try?"

"Because your aim is to destroy all life and everything good upon the worlds."

"Oh, there are so many vices to which you can give that label. Fear, for example. Not to mention entropy."

I really didn't want to be having a conversation with the greatest possible source of evil. I tried to turn away, but wherever I looked the great darkened ball stood in front of me. It generated static that pulled on my fur, and that constant stench of yeast extract – let's just say that I can think of only one thing worse than consuming rotten vegetable juice.

"What do you want?" I asked.

"Merely to remind you that your time is nigh. I am here now, in the dream realm. I am watching, and I am growing."

"Ah ha, so still within a *woken* dream ... I'm not dead."

"Not yet, Dragoncat. But now you have entered here you cannot escape. These dreams will kill you eventually. Unless ... close your eyes, Dragoncat. I can save you from death."

A plume of purple smoke drifted up from my feet. It washed against my fur, seeming to cleanse it. The weakness evaporated from my muscles, and a sweetness filled my nostrils. A sense of belonging. A sense of power ...

I closed my eyes, ready to accept it. I really had no choice.

"No!"

My eyes jolted open. Was that the voice of my crystal? It had a Welsh accent, yet it was slightly smoother still.

Something shimmered behind the form of the globe of floating darkness. A vision of someone beautiful emerged, her long golden hair swaying in an invisible breeze.

"You," *Cana Dei* said.

But as she crystallised further, the giant goddess Brigit wasn't focused on the darkness. Rather her eyes – fires burning behind them – looked right down upon me.

"This dream is not for you, Dragoncat. Go and join your friends, and I will deal with the darkness."

"You cannot—"

Brigit swept her arm in a wide circle, cutting off *Cana Dei's* complaint and sending out a flurry of what looked like crisp autumn leaves. They hit me hard on the face, and then I saw darkness once again, followed by a bright light.

Brigit's voice trailed behind me.

"You must learn to navigate the dreams, Dragoncat, or they will destroy you."

Then I was magically lifted off my feet once again.

27

A TERRIBLY FAMILIAR DREAM

The dream tunnel sent me plunging, whipping, and flailing through rings of light. But this time I wasn't complaining. Multiple times I'd thought I'd died, and *Cana Dei* had tried to swallow me into its own version of oblivion, but Brigit had saved me.

I was still alive, and I still had control of my mind. That was something to be grateful for.

I tumbled out into a realm that smelled of eggs and rotten vegetable juice. The sky was as bleak as it always was in the Darklands, and the land so cracked and split that purple gas leached out from everywhere as if from the planet's core.

Nothing living grew here. Nor were there any magical creations within sight. The land looked drier than an elephant's desert graveyard; where warlocks practiced their magic, nothing else could thrive.

A single hovel lay at the edge of the horizon, painted such a bright red that it stuck out like a welt. Seramina was sitting in a bamboo rocking chair behind a balustrade on the porch, her silver hair lit purple by the glowing mists.

She held her staff, the crystal glowing bright white. Even

from this distance, I could see how her eyes blazed white. Esme sat on one side of her, Max on the other. But they didn't seem to be moving. They had their heads craned up towards the magic coming out of Seramina's staff.

Something wasn't right here …

It took me a while to remember that I'd seen this before, except without Esme and Max. The Ghost Realm had revealed it to us all as a vision – the day that Seramina defeated the warlocks, the day that she destroyed the worlds. I'd seen her tear the earth asunder and summon all the demons from the Seventh Dimension. In destroying the warlocks, she'd created her own personal apocalypse.

I didn't waste a moment, but sprinted over to her. A strong wind ruffled my fur.

"Seramina," I said as I skidded to a halt, kicking up the dust behind me and releasing sulphur from beneath the soil. "What are you doing?"

"Do not try to stop me, Ben," Seramina said. "The warlocks are coming, and I will finish them. This is my chance to defeat them."

I turned my gaze towards Max and Esme – they looked like statues. Seramina had used her magic to freeze them to the spot.

"Seramina, you have to stop this. This isn't the way—"

Whiskers, I hoped she hadn't encountered *Cana Dei* too. I hoped it hadn't taken control of her mind. I couldn't bear being forced to fight Seramina again. Besides, without Esme here to help, I knew I didn't stand a chance.

"Ben, they are coming—" she said it through clenched teeth, "—and if I stop them here then I will save the dimensions."

"But why like this?" I asked. "What did you do to Max and Esme?"

"I will do it to you too if you stand in my way, Dragoncat. Now step aside."

I growled a rebuke as I turned around. If anything went wrong, then I'd better be able to react while not rendered completely inert.

There came a screech from the sky, followed by grunts and wheezes and screams. Six birds of prey darted out of the clouds. A condor, a buzzard, a bald eagle, a hawk, a seagull, and a vulture, all flying in one direction. The air for a moment stank of bird sweat.

"It's time." Seramina stood up, kicking the rocking chair behind her.

The hovel, the porch, and the chair suddenly winked out of existence, disappearing into the space that separates dreams. The warlocks in their bird forms let out their terrifying cries, and I braced myself for a fight.

❧ 28 ❧

THE WORLD ASUNDER

The warlocks, still in their bird-of-prey forms, approached us from the sky.

The Darklands brimmed with dangerous magic and tangible silence. The warlocks had cleared this land, ready for the encounter that we'd all seen visions of – the inevitable future that none of us could escape. Now either they would destroy the worlds, or Seramina would.

The silver-haired teenager grasped her staff in both hands and raised it high above her head. The warlocks landed each in turn, sending up six thick puffs of feathers and smoke. Their human forms emerged from the fumes.

The condor, Lasinta the ancient lady, their leader. The bald eagle, Moonz, Lasinta's only slightly younger peer – a wrinkled old man yet sturdier in build than Lasinta. The vulture, tall and lanky Junas, bald with a hooked nose. The buzzard, Ritrad, the youngest and most muscular. The white seagull, Cala, the only one of the sextet whom humans might consider conventionally beautiful, with red hair almost as brilliant as Asinda's. The hawk, Pladana, a small and wiry woman.

Once they had fully transformed into humans, the warlocks fanned out, their staffs at the ready.

Lasinta stepped to the front.

"What do you want, Lasinta?" Seramina said, her eyes blazing with amber fire. "All of you ... why do you disturb me? All I ever wanted is to be left alone."

She'd recited it word for word, just had she had spoken in the vision. She definitely knew her part. It occurred to me that this might not be the real Seramina, but a version of her in someone else's dream.

Yet I had found my way to different versions of Ben the Dragoncat, and I somehow knew Seramina would find her way here. She'd been seeking this destiny for a long, long time.

"You hold too much power," Lasinta replied. "Not only are you a threat to our kind, but you can help us break the treaty with Illumine Kingdom and finish what Astravar started, fool as that man was. This is your last chance. You either join us, or it all ends here."

I shuddered as I considered calling upon my staff bearer. But I figured Seramina would see that as an intrusion, and I needed control over my own faculties. She was more powerful than I, and if I tried turning into a chimera, I had no doubt she'd turn me into a fly or a frog or another type of horrid creature that a cat should never become.

Instead I edged nearer to Lasinta, so I could see her up close. Neither she nor Seramina paid me any heed. After all, I wasn't meant to be in this dream, and so I couldn't disturb it just by being here.

Seramina lifted her staff even higher, and the ground shook. I hissed, crouched, and dug my claws into the soil, tearing up clods of earth.

"I owe you nothing, Lasinta," Seramina said. "My father is dead, and you will soon be too if you don't leave this place."

Seramina swung her staff in a downwards arc. As if anticipating the move, Lasinta screamed out and angled the end of her staff outwards. Two dragons made entirely of purple mist spun out of the crystal on the elderly warlock's staff, screeching as they spiralled around in the air.

Behind all this, the other warlocks cast spells of their own. Beams of all different colours traced into the sky and the landscape stank like a thousand manure pits topped with rotten vegetables.

The warlocks' spells gathered mass, and then in one giant ball they headed towards Seramina. Lasinta's wispy dragons circled the ball, their eyes set on the teenager.

I knew what would come next: Seramina would thrust her staff into the ground and rend the earth apart. Demons would spout from the cracks, released and ready to conquer the worlds.

Except I realised what was wrong – the woman at the front of the formation didn't have a deeply wrinkled face and wilting hair. Instead, her skin was freckly and young, and her hair was the colour of brilliant fire.

This wasn't Lasinta's dream after all, but our friend Asinda's. She turned to look down at me with her bright cornflower eyes.

"Ben?" she asked. "What are you doing here?"

Meanwhile, I could see the intent burning in the fires at the back of Seramina's eyes. If she woke Asinda up, then we wouldn't be able to recruit her help. Even worse, the demons might kill us, and who would be left to fight the warlocks then?

The silver-haired teenager brought her staff downwards.

"Seramina, stop!" I shouted.

"I told you not to interfere," she screamed.

"But this isn't even Lasinta's dream ... look who you're fighting, Seramina. It's Asinda."

Seramina's staff plunged into the ground, and the earth

shook violently, sending out a roar like overhead thunder. Fissures shot out across the rocky ground, sending out great streams of dust. Heat surrounded us.

Then, from the cracks in the earth, swarmed the demons: first came the demon rats, chittering to the rhythm of the crackling fire within their bodies. A menagerie of demon beasts followed – crocodiles, wildebeest, rabbits, flamingos, crows. It didn't matter how fierce or gentle their real-world counterparts might be; all of these beasts looked terrifying, with the way the lava glowed beneath their craggy skin. The smell of rotten vegetable juice was replaced with that of fiery brimstone.

The demons scanned the world around them, looking for something to destroy. The burning eyes of a demon latched onto me.

"Asinda?" Seramina said. "I've just found my way into this dream. What's going on?"

"You're trying to destroy us!" I said. "You froze Esme and Max to the spot."

"Not me ... a version of me in this dream. It's Asinda's?"

"It's too late," I cried. "We need to get out of here."

"I can fight them," Asinda cried. "I can help them."

"No, don't ..." I said. "You can't die here, Asinda, but we can."

She narrowed her eyes. "What do you mean?"

There came a roar from the demon dragon that had identified me as a target. It turned around to face me. Demon dragons have no jaws – their mouths remain always open. But some dangerous vacuum deep inside their rocky forms causes them to suck in air and everything else from the ground.

"You must come to the Faerie Realm, Asinda," I said. "Go to the top of the Tower of the Grand and the Oracle Fairy will open a portal for you."

"The Tower of the Grand? But it's been under heavy

guard since— Wait, if this is a dream, this has to be nonsense."

I really didn't have the patience for this. "You will find a way, Asinda. You must ..."

I didn't have any more time. The demon dragon had entered a dive and it bore down upon me. It would swallow me whole in its great gaping mouth if I didn't do something.

I summoned my staff bearer, and this time it placed a very solid staff between my jaws. Energy surged into my muscles. My staff burned at the back of my mouth.

"*So you return,*" said the voice of *Cana Dei* inside my head. But I ignored it.

Instead, I shot out a beam of red magic. My intent was to destroy. I fired it straight at Asinda.

"Ben, what are you doing?"

"Go to the Tower of the Grand, Asinda," I said.

Immediately, the demon dragon sucked me into its mouth. But I had already woken Asinda, and so I fell out of her dream.

29

THE FIRE WITHIN A DREAM

I found myself in the tunnel of light once again. I wasn't flailing around hopelessly this time, but swimming the pathways like a salmon in a stream. I'd seen something like this in my dreams before, and I imagined myself surrounded by a school of friendly fish.

Kick tail. Turn dorsal fin. Let myself sail through the light, until I find a suitable location – a waterfall that I need to leap.

I had worked out how to navigate the dreams. All I had to do was find a version of Ben that somebody was dreaming of. To achieve success, I needed to find a dream in which I wasn't about to die.

But I also needed to find a dream which contained Seramina, Max, and Esme so I could talk to them. We needed to work out what to do next.

As I whirled through the dream tunnel I scanned the ocean beneath me, looking for possibilities. Visions of different dreams flashed by. I saw Elysian fields rich with pollen, kites made from wood and papyrus, honey dripping off a fat honeycomb, and lighthouses, treehouses, and whirlwinds.

Then I saw the dream I needed, a campfire on a full-mooned night. Before I had even entered the dream, I could feel the fire's warmth drenching my pores and smell the mutton sausages cooking within the smoke.

I let myself go, surrendering every single muscle. I floated down into nothingness as the world flashed light, then dark, and finally revealed the scene.

It smelled delicious. There seemed to be a thousand mutton sausages turning on a spit over the fire. They turned of their own accord – no one needed to take a position on the crank handle. Esme, Max, and Seramina sat together on a log on one side of the fire. Behind it, the Willowed Woods crept up into the sky – their spindly branches seeming to shimmer in the slits of moonlight that found their way through.

On another log sat Rine in a blue vest and blue trousers, with Ange nestled in one of his arms. And I say one of his arms, because he had another girl in his other arm, with golden blonde hair. I didn't need to sniff the air for long to recognise the heady perfume of strawberries and cream – Bellari's signature fragrance. Ange wore an olive-green blouse and a short skirt, and Bellari wore the same, except in scarlet.

Whiskers, in his dream Rine had decided to court them both. It made me seethe inside.

"Rine, you're so handsome," Ange said as she fondled his chin. "How did I ever manage to find a boyfriend as awesome as you?"

"You know, I've always loved you," Bellari said from her position against Rine's shoulder. "But you can have two girl-friends because you deserve it, you know. Rine ... after everything you've done for me, and everything you've done for Ange ... you're so special, Rine."

Whiskers, I didn't like this one bit. I knew it was a dream and all that, but really? What was wrong with this boy?

I decided dream or no dream that I couldn't let Rine get

away with this. He loved Ange, not Bellari. I couldn't risk bringing that red-faced fire mage back into my life again.

I rushed over to Rine and leaped up onto his knee. Then I turned to Bellari and brushed against her hair, making sure that a good bit of dander rubbed off onto her. I shook my fur as if shaking off water for extra effect. You know, they say Bengals are hypoallergenic, so I don't know what all this nonsense with Bellari and her allergies was about.

"Hello, Bellari," I said. "Fancy seeing you here."

She lifted her head, and then she did something completely unexpected. Instead of coughing, sneezing, and screaming at me, she beamed a wide smile.

"Oh, it's been so long. I've missed you, Ben. Come to Auntie Bellari, you cute little kitty."

She extended her forefinger and scratched me gently on the head with her nail. It felt so tender ... but I didn't like it one bit. This wasn't how Bellari was meant to behave.

"That's it, Bellari," Rine said. "I told you he was okay."

But I wasn't okay at that moment – I wasn't okay with this at all.

I swiped away Bellari's hand with a sharp claw, then I backed up against Ange, who sucked in an agitated breath right next to my ear. In a second, she leaped off the log and screamed at me at such a high pitch, I barely managed to flatten my ears in time to stop my eardrums from bursting.

"Get away from me, Ben," Ange said. Her face had gone red underneath her short brown hair. "You know I can't handle this ... I'm allergic."

"Now, now, Ange, that's Bellari's line," Rine said. "Isn't it, buttercup?"

"She can have it," Bellari said and giggled. "She can take any line she wants. While she does that, I'm going to become High Prefect. You do know they'll make me High Prefect, don't you, Rine? That's what mother's always wanted. I hear she set up a fund that will allow me to sail to the top. That way, she'll set me up for a good career when I finally ..."

I didn't stick around longer to find out what she'd say next. I was right off Rine's lap and hiding on the other side of the fire. The embers crackled loudly enough that I couldn't hear any more of their nonsense.

I found a mutton sausage on the floor there, so I sniffed it cautiously and took a few nibbles from it. It tasted good, but I soon realised it wouldn't satisfy my hunger. After all, this was just a dream.

"You should leave Rine alone," Esme said. "We don't want to wake him up right now, do we? Not when we've found a place where we can sit and discuss the plan."

"But have you seen what he's doing? He's with both Bellari and Ange, and he's made Ange the bad one. This isn't right!"

"Oh, let him have his fun," Esme said. "He's only dreaming."

"And don't tell Ange about this dream," Seramina said. "She won't appreciate it, I'm telling you."

"I like the blonde one," Max barked, as though he understood everything we were talking about. "She's very friendly."

"Have you forgotten that she hates you in the real world, Max?" I asked. "She dates boys with very big feet and orders them to kick any creature that doesn't stand above her knees."

"Yes, but she gave me a sausage here," Max said. "Good people give you sausages; bad people don't. It's a law of nature."

I walked up to Seramina and sat on her lap. Even though this was a dream, she still smelled distinctly of her snowdrop perfume, and she remained characteristically calm.

It didn't matter that she'd almost destroyed me in the last dream. It hadn't really been her anyway. The real Seramina wouldn't have behaved that way – not after the experience she'd had with *Cana Dei* at the Altar of Lore, when she'd let it in during a battle against the warlocks and it had almost destroyed her soul.

I rested a moment, purring as Seramina tickled the back of my neck. Everyone seemed to need to rest, actually. I guessed that *Cana Dei* might have taken Max, Esme, and Seramina through the same treatment as me – almost killing them in each dream, and then trying to convince them there was a better way. What was *Cana Dei* doing here, anyway? It belonged in the Ghost Realm, and not in the world of dreams. Or perhaps it lived here too? I really had no idea.

The warmth from the fire washed over me. Between the cracklings of the fire, I could hear Bellari's giggles, Ange's coos, and Rine's boasts about what a 'fine figure of a man' he was. I was starting to feel nauseous just listening to it.

Instead, I thought it better to break the silence.

"So now we're all here," I said. "I told Asinda in that last vision to climb the Tower of the Grand, before Seramina almost fried us all."

"It wasn't me ..." Seramina said. "I'm sorry, I just came so late. I got a little lost in the dream world. I saw ... it doesn't matter ... I just don't know why Asinda was dreaming about that horrible moment. It's meant to be *my* destiny."

"I just hope she listened about coming to find us. I mean, do you do what people tell you to do in your dreams?"

Esme stalked over and put her paws on Seramina's lap, so her head rested just next to mine. I could hear her purring. I guess we all needed comfort right now.

"Asinda's smart," Esme said. "She'll know that something was different about that dream – just like you did when you first met Seramina."

"Yes, but will she listen?" I asked.

"We will see," Esme said.

"And yet," I said, "we still need to find Lasinta and

discover what she's up to. But how are we ever going to find her?"

"Well," Seramina said. "I've been thinking about that."

She leaned forwards to stand up. Esme and I both scrambled off her lap. The teenager reached behind her back and drew out her staff, though it soon became apparent she didn't intend to use it for magic.

Instead, she placed it on the ground and hunched herself over it. She looked the perfect imitation of an old woman as she hobbled over to Rine, the staff wobbling as it supported her weight.

"Coo-ee, Rine," she said in a croaky voice.

Rine turned his head and his jaw fell slightly.

"Seramina," he said. "No, not today. You don't belong in this dream, I'm afraid."

"Oh, but I'm not Seramina, dear. My name is Lasinta. The old warlock, don't you know me?"

"Lasinta? Heavens, yeah, I know you. But not now – I don't want you in this dream. Buzz off ... please."

"There's no need to be so rude, Rine," Ange said.

"Yeah," Bellari said. "We can all be friends. Me, you, Ange, the animals, and this old warlock ..."

"What are you talking about?" Rine asked. "We can't be friends with Lasinta. She's not even here."

"Oh, but she is here," Seramina said, still using that croaky voice. "Look over there."

She pointed into the darkness with her staff. Rine squinted his eyes.

"What? There's nothing there."

"Are you sure, Rine?" Seramina said. "Because I can see her, and I think Ange and Bellari can too."

"Yeah, I see her," Ange said.

"Me too," Bellari said.

"What? Where? Wait a minute," he put his hand over his eyes and peered out. "Wait, yes, I see her."

The elderly warlock appeared in the gloom, fringed by a curtain of white light. She stopped and looked around, and I heard her muttering.

"Another dream. No, this one is useless."

"Ladies, stay right there," Rine said. "Your hero High Prefect Rine will deal with the old warlock."

"No, you won't," Seramina said, and her voice was laced with command. "Stay right there, Rine, and you can wake up in ten seconds."

She pointed her staff at the boy and a spark of lightning flashed out of it and hit him on the forehead. Rine spasmed for a moment, then he froze to the spot. Bellari and Ange suddenly disappeared from view.

Seramina looked back at Lasinta, who was turning slowly away. Her body was fading. If we didn't act fast, we'd lose her.

"We've got her," Seramina said. She stretched out her staff in front of her and held it out horizontally with both hands. Her arms formed a cradle.

"We must move fast," she said. "Jump on, Max—"

Max barked. He seemed to understand everything we said in this place, but then that was the nature of dreams. With astonishing dexterity, he jumped up and folded himself out over Seramina's arms. He sat there, wagging his tail, his long tongue lolling out in front of him.

"What about us?" I asked.

"Hold on to my arms," Seramina said. "Quickly."

"What? How? We don't have fingers to grip onto you with ..."

"Our staff bearers," Esme said.

She summoned hers from thin air. This time, the white hand wasn't holding her staff, and it wasn't gigantic but normal human-sized. It grasped onto one of Seramina's forearms.

"Ben, quick," Seramina said. "We'll lose her."

I growled; I never like to be hurried. But I knew she was right, and so I also summoned my staff bearer, making sure I imagined it without a staff. The white hand appeared, again as a normal human-sized hand. It clutched onto Seramina's other forearm. I felt a tightness in my right forepaw, almost as if it were me clinging onto her.

"Now," Seramina said, "we follow. Hold on tight and don't get thrown off."

She leaped up into the air and together we flew.

30

CHASING BIN BAGS

Part of me had had enough of these tunnels of light. It really took it out of you being flung around from dream to dream – no wonder you woke up tired after a slew of night-mares. I just wanted to be back in Salanraja's chamber, eating a giant dragon-breath-roasted fish off the floor stones, and I wouldn't complain that it wasn't salmon.

I know that I said I wanted to forget about food, but a cat can only go hungry for so long.

But then, another part of me felt grateful that I no longer had to navigate the dreams alone. Seramina had now taken the helm, her arms stretched out and holding her staff in front of her like a steering wheel.

Max sat upon her arms, facing into the wind, which was brushing back his fur, and panting happily. Both Esme and I had our staff bearers – the now human-sized white hands without our staffs – clinging onto her for dear life.

I doubt they hung on for their own lives though. While I knew very little about the origin and nature of these staff bearers, I had a strong hunch they were immortal. I didn't even know from whence they came. I imagined there was another dimension filled with giant hands, waiting patiently for someone to summon them and give them a purpose.

After all, I used to believe that there was only one world – my comfortable home in South Wales. Since then I'd learned there were eight of them, not to mention the dream world that linked all our minds together.

As Seramina flew, the two white hands pulled Esme and me along using invisible bonds that couldn't be broken. I didn't feel like I was being dragged, though. Rather, it felt like being propelled along by strong currents of water or being swept upon a strong wind.

I'd learned from experience to just relax into such things. So, although my tummy rumbled as if its inner linings were having seismic difficulties, I grumbled to no one – not even myself.

Seramina was chasing a shadow. It wasn't easy to see in the shimmering pulses of light that flooded the tunnel, but still, if I squinted my eyes I could see Lasinta's hunched form navigating the pathways like a dustbin bag floating on heavy winds.

Beneath us, dreams flitted through the oceans, and with every wave there came a new one. I saw blackberries and thorns, clouds and thunder, a panther stalking through the trees, and a boy wearing only leaves chasing after it.

I didn't just see human dreams; I saw cat dreams, dog dreams, fairy dreams. Demon dreams, dragon dreams, unicorn dreams. The only dreams I didn't see were crystal dreams – but then crystals aren't living creatures, after all.

Suddenly, the shadow of Lasinta veered sharply off to the left and dived down into the ocean. Seramina and Max went under the surface, and our staff bearers pulled Esme and me through soon after.

There was a crash and then an icy chill. For a moment I couldn't breathe, yet still Seramina dived deeper – through the true tapestry of dreams. They spun past me as if a baby had got hold of the remote control for the television – endlessly flicking from channel to channel. Would there be any end to this?

We crashed even deeper through another surface, and back into an open space. We landed on soft ground, and I lifted my head to see all six of the warlocks standing around a burning brazier, otherwise surrounded by darkness.

They looked as if they were preparing for war.

SCHEMES

T he brazier burned brightly, sending out a circle of light over the red, sandy ground. It played patterns of shadows over the figures of the six warlocks, deepening the wrinkles on Lasinta and Moonz's faces, and making Cala's usually pristine cheeks seem harsh and pockmarked. It sent up such a thick soup of smoke that I wondered if we might die here from suffocation.

But I knew that all six of these warlocks needed to stay alive also, as they were no doubt in a *woken* dream. They weren't going to conjure up anything that could kill anyone – or at least I hoped they wouldn't.

Seramina had landed us in the shadows, amidst some fresh clumps of grass. My paws sank into the soft mud beneath them, which cooled them somewhat. I doubted that the warlocks would be able to see us, but at the same time I could feel ants crawling through my fur.

Despite this I stayed as still as a gargoyle. Seramina dropped Max on the ground, and in the thin light I gave him a glare to tell him not to dare bark. He whimpered softly, and I worried that even that might be enough to alert the warlocks to our presence.

"Should we attack?" I asked. "Perhaps the four of us could take them."

"Not a chance," Seramina said. "Not without Asinda ... I don't want to risk any of us dying."

"And what do you think, Esme?" I asked.

Esme was also powerful, but still not a patch on Seramina at full stretch. I doubted she was as powerful as Lasinta either, but perhaps she could convince Seramina to aid us.

"She's right," Esme whispered in the human language. "We need to know exactly what they're planning."

"Just stay absolutely still," Seramina said. "The warlocks know we shouldn't be in this dream."

"But whose dream is it?" I asked.

"It doesn't matter," Esme said. "Now hush."

I realised that one of the warlocks had to be sleeping for the others to visit this dream. He or she must have had the ability to control their own dreams and imagine the other five warlocks around the brazier. Or perhaps one of them slept while another whispered exactly what was to happen in the sleeping warlock's ear. I'd seen such things happening in cartoons on the television back in South Wales.

I tried to keep as low a profile as possible. We all did, in fact. If the warlocks discovered our presence they could simply eject us, and we probably wouldn't have an opportunity to eavesdrop on them like this.

I perked up my ears so I could listen to the warlocks. Out of the corner of my eye, I noticed Esme doing the same. Max lay down low in the grass, sniffing at something, but not even letting out a whisper. He looked wiser somewhat, as if he'd gained a power of his own through his dreamwalking. But I didn't have a chance to discover what that might be.

Seramina had her staff laid out in front of her in the grass, clutching it tightly at the base with both hands. The crystal on it shimmered faintly, casting a spell that made it easier for her to hear exactly what the warlocks said.

"It's a shame we couldn't all meet in the Wastelands," the tall lanky warlock, Junas, said. "I don't like the dangers involved in *woken* dreams."

"You know full well that I don't have time to travel to the First Dimension," Lasinta said. "If I do that, I lose control of the fairies."

"But do not despair," the elderly man, Moonz interposed. "Soon, our dear leader will command the fairies to open a portal for us all and then we can make a new base in the Second Dimension. There's so much more magic there that we can exploit."

Murmurs of approval came from around the fireplace. Naked tree stumps suddenly appeared between the warlocks and the brazier. A silver goblet rested upon each one. Lasinta leaned forward and picked up her goblet. The other warlocks followed suit, and together they raised the cups in the air and took a sip.

From the circle drifted heady scents of wine – I've never understood why humans like the drink so much. I mean, how could they even like grapes?

"So has anyone discovered anything of interest?" Lasinta asked. "Because I myself have found some interesting links."

"Oh do tell, Lasinta," Moonz said. He leaned forwards, and his aged brows furrowed deeply.

"I think I've found the link between the dragons of the academy," Lasinta said. "It was so obvious that I can't believe we didn't see it sooner. Who else would they all connect to, but the oldest and wisest dragon of them all?"

"I found it too," Cala said. "The white dragon Olan ... Aleam's dragon ... she's the key."

"Exactly," Lasinta said, and she clapped her hands together. "If we can control her mind through the dreams, we can get other dragons to follow. A simple bit of dream hypnosis through magic and ancient ritual, and we'll get all the dragons to submit to our cause."

"And we can then use that link to control the king's dragon," Pladana said. "This is brilliant, Lasinta. We can seize control of the First Dimension."

Lasinta's lips curled upwards into a wicked grin. "Then, once we have done that, we can work on the unicorns, or perhaps even the great bronze dragon trainer, Matharon." She steepled her fingers underneath her chin. "So the question is, where shall we perform the ritual?"

"How does it work, again?" Ritrad asked. "I'm a bit sketchy on the details. You had a name for it?"

The bald-headed muscular warlock was the youngest, which I guess made him the least in the know.

Moonz looked at him. "It's the Ritual of Arcanas. And you still have a lot to learn, young warlock."

Ritrad lowered his head. "I know," he said.

"No matter," Moonz said. "We haven't time to chastise you right now. Just know that on the evening the full moon rises, just as the sun falls beneath the horizon, all crystals are charged with great power. In most dimensions, this doesn't happen often. But in the Faerie Realm it happens every month."

"So, do we have a crystal set up?" Ritrad asked.

"Indeed we do," Moonz said. "One of the grandest crystals of them all is currently being stolen away by our fairies. We only need a place where we can perform the ritual undisturbed."

"I've already thought ahead for that one," Pladana said, shifting her wiry frame. "I have sent watchers ahead to the Aisean Wetlands – they used to be Astravar's pets. Well, let's just say I salvaged some of his magic."

The Aisean Wetlands ... Ca'mun, the fairy queen, had

mentioned them. She'd said there were a lot of crows there who would be happy to have a meal of beetles delivered to them. These must be the 'watchers' Pladana had referred to. So they were under the control of the warlocks – somehow, I wasn't surprised.

Lasinta cackled so loudly that I was startled for a moment. "Just imagine how the First Dimension will crumble after we control the dragons," she said. "That girl, Seramina – I would never have to fight her. I know she will kill me eventually, but if we preserve her in magic, she won't have to do so for tens of thousands of years. It's a shame, really; I always thought that we could have converted those four young dark mages to our cause."

"That will never happen," Pladana said. "They have too many allies in high circles – Immortals and the like."

Lasinta gazed into the distance. "No, I guess it won't. Fortunately for us, we only need to preserve the life of the daughter of Astravar, or at least we need to do so for all of us to live. My grandniece, Asinda, the dog, and the two cats: we will end them."

Whiskers, I wasn't liking this one bit. Clearly Lasinta knew about this vision involving Seramina, and she seemed to think that it was definitely going to happen. If you couldn't block destiny, then at least you can delay it.

A deep growl came from my chest, and I hadn't realised I was doing it until Esme turned her narrow eyes toward me.

"Shut up, Ben," she said.

"Yes, shut up," Max barked.

All of us looked at him sharply, but it was too late.

"Wait a minute, do you hear that?" Lasinta asked.

"Just a dog," Junas said. "Nothing to worry about."

"Not something to worry about?" Cala said. "I didn't plant any dogs in Pladana's head ... there shouldn't be anything but the six of us, the fire, and the wine in this dream."

Lasinta stood up and drew her staff from her back. "Battle stations, we've been compromised."

"I see them," Moonz said, also drawing his staff. "There in the grass."

"Yes," Lasinta said, and her staff glowed a bright purple. A massive ball of electricity shot out of it, heading straight towards us. Hackles shot out of my back, and I felt the static pulling at every single hair on my body.

"Oh no you don't," boomed a deep and sonorous voice from in front of us. It sounded like a thousand cats sharpening their claws at the same time.

Lasinta's spell hit a solid yet invisible wall in front of us and exploded. I yowled as a sudden and intense heat washed over my fur. But it didn't last long enough to cause any damage.

Some of the light from the explosion remained, highlighting a massive tree stretching up towards sparks of lightning in the sky. A giant ash tree – *Fraxinus Maximus*. The Oracle Fairy had come to rescue us.

"*Yggdrasil,*" Lasinta said. "So it's you who's aided them. And to think I suspected Bastet."

"You shall not harm them," the Oracle Fairy said. "They are under my ward."

"Then it's you who shall be the first to perish by dragonfire. We will hunt you down to the end of the worlds if we have to. In the meantime, come to the agreed upon location, warlocks. Tonight is the night we perform the ritual."

"Tonight," the warlocks chanted in unison. "The ritual of Arcanas, tonight..."

Together, the fire, the goblets, and the warlocks winked out of existence. But instead of being drawn back into the dream tunnels, I felt water against my fur and heard the nearby splashing of a waterfall. The spray continued to ruffle my fur.

"It's time to awaken, young ones," the Oracle Fairy said.

I opened my eyes to find myself inside the pond at the base of the cascade, the bright glow that had suffused the water now fading.

On the fairy dust beach, a young lady awaited us whom I was incredibly glad to see.

'BEEF JOIKY'

The red-haired Asinda looked out at us from the golden, shiny beach with her cornflower eyes. She wore the armour of a dragon rider – burnished leather covering her chest and thighs, and yellow leather pauldrons on her shoulders. A red cloak denoted her school of magic as a fire mage, even if Asinda was technically a dark magician. But over this she also wore a white shawl that I guess indicated her as being a member of the School of the White.

Asinda's dragon, Shadorow, lay in the sand next to her. He was a charcoal dragon, with greyish-black scales the colour of shale. He was also one of the most agile dragons to have come out of Dragonsbond Academy, which suited Asinda's monkey-like flexibility very well. As the story goes, Shadorow had saved Asinda from a nasty fall while climbing in the Crystal Mountains back in the First Dimension. The two had been bonded ever since.

Above the duo, the sun had begun its descent in the sky. Its colour was transitioning from bright white to a softer yellow.

The water felt refreshingly cool, and part of me wanted to

stay swimming in it all day – particularly after having almost died so many times in the dream world – and then go to sleep on the beach. But I knew we had work to do.

"Asinda!" Seramina shouted.

The younger teenager seemed to have forgotten she couldn't swim and kicked her way to the bank. Perhaps she had learned how to do so in the dream – while my friends were busy killing me, they'd been giving Seramina swimming lessons.

As soon as she left the water, Seramina's swimsuit vanished, to be replaced by her chiffon dress. Clearly glamour magic was still involved, since although Seramina's dress wasn't soaked, rivulets of water still streamed off her pale hair and skin.

Asinda smiled at Seramina, who threw her arms around her in a hug.

"Seramina, you're all wet," Asinda said.

"Yes, this is revenge for dreaming of me. I didn't confide in you about that vision in the Ghost Realm so you could almost kill me in it."

"Kill you?" Asinda asked.

"We've been dreamwalking. The Oracle Fairy showed the others how. But you know what happens when we die in a *woken* dream."

"Well, I had kind of figured," Asinda said. "That's why I came ... I sensed something was different about you and Ben. He wouldn't have normally walked up to me like that ... not in that specific dream."

Seramina looked down at me and smiled, as if to say thank you. "Anyway, how are you, Asinda? It feels like ages. How are things in the Dragon Guard? How's Lars, for that matter?"

"Lars is ..." Asinda lowered her head and hesitated. "Well,

he's Lars. Always a hero." And she didn't seem to want to elaborate on that.

As the two reunited friends chinwagged, I swam my way towards the shore. Esme had already reached it, and by the time I emerged she was grooming the water off her fur. I did the same. The water had a slight brackish quality to it; strangely, it was slightly peppery as well.

Max reached the shore last, and he shook his body so hard that we all got covered in spray. Asinda looked down at him and snarled.

"*Dogs*," she said.

"Dogs, yourself!" Max barked back.

I turned sharply towards the dog. "Wait ... what? You understand?"

"I met my crystal in the dream world," Max said. "It gave me the gift of all languages like you have. Now I can understand you."

"Great," I said. "So now you can tell Asinda what you really think."

"No, I won't. I won't speak anything but the dog language. It's the dog code."

"Wonderful," Esme said. "He can understand everything we say, and we'll have to listen to him barking his head off over every detail."

"Don't be so insulting," Max barked.

"Esme's always insulting," I snapped back. "You're going to need to get used to it."

"That's a curse, not a gift! My crystal gave me a curse!"

"Max, stop complaining." I looked up at Asinda and then I asked in the human language, "Have you got any food to shut the Sussex spaniel up?"

Asinda grinned. "As a matter of fact, I have."

She reached into the pouch on her waist and produced

some thin brown strips. She threw one down on the ground in front of Max.

"This is a delicacy from the Fourth Dimension – a gift from the king's envoys there that they gave to all new recruits in the Dragon Guard. They call it 'beef joiky' I believe." She didn't actually say 'beef joiky' in the language of the First Dimension, but in the one from the Fourth Dimension known as English.

"Beef joiky," Seramina repeated, rolling the words around on her tongue.

Max already had some in his mouth. "It's good," he said in the dog language – because he refused to speak anything else. "I've had this before."

Asinda threw another strip down on the ground in front of me, and one in front of Esme. Max tried to move in on my strip, but I showed him my full extent of my teeth and raised a paw. The old Ragamuffin back in my neighbourhood had a saying – wise dogs know never to steal food off a cat. It's the foolish ones who get scratched.

Fortunately Max seemed wise enough to leave my food alone.

I sniffed at the food. "Why does this beef smell of sugar?" I asked.

"That's part of the appeal," Asinda said, handing another strip to Seramina.

"It's good, Ben," Esme said in the cat language, between chewing. "Try it."

"Fine," I said. "But if I don't like it, I'm going into the forest to hunt a rabbit."

"You'll like it Ben, I promise."

I sniffed at it again, then touched it with my paw. Then it got covered in sand, so I had to toss it around, but that only made it worse.

"You've ruined it!" Max said. "I should have just eaten it myself."

"Shut up," I said, and picked it up in my mouth.

I expected the fairy dust to make it gritty, but rather it seemed to smooth the texture of the meat. It even added a slightly nutty-spicy flavour to it. I guess it was a bit like paprika.

"Good, right?" Esme said.

"It's okay," I said. "I prefer smoked salmon. And we've still not had any mutton sausage – what happened to dragon rider tradition?"

"You did have some, in the dream realm," Esme pointed out. "But you didn't seem to want to eat much."

"After seeing Bellari being weird like that, I felt a little nauseous. Plus, that mutton sausage wasn't real food, it was dream food. It won't fill my tummy, and neither will a few scraps of 'beef joiky'."

Asinda laughed, as if she understood. Other than the fact I'd said 'beef joiky' in the human language of the Fourth Dimension, there was no way she could have interpreted the rest of my and Esme's dialogue of chirps unless her crystal had also given her the gift of all languages, too. I guess she just found it 'cute', as humans tend to. They seemed to enjoy listening to us talk to each other.

"Do you want some more, Ben?" Asinda asked.

My tummy rumbled to tell me yes. So I meowed like a cat, without needing to translate into human. That was another universal law of cats that I'd learned from the old Ragamuffin; he had called it Ragamuffin's Third Law – cuteness beats language every time.

Asinda threw two more scraps down each for me, Esme, and Max and also gave another few scraps to Seramina. This time I wolfed them down before the sand could get to them. I wanted to experience the real thing, and also, I didn't want the fairy dust messing with my head. Not after what had happened in Dragonsbond Academy.

Just as I was chewing the last tiny bit, the Oracle Fairy called down to us: "If you're quite finished down there, we have important tasks to be discussing."

Esme and I looked at each other, and we both licked our lips. Then we raced each other to the top of the cliff.

PLANS

I don't know how he managed it, but Max overtook us on our way up to the clifftop where the Oracle Fairy towered high. The Sussex spaniel turned his head to us as if to gloat, but the looks both Esme and I gave him must have made him think better of it.

The soft grass moved beneath my paws, and my fur wicked dewdrops off the tall blades. The sun was now falling much faster, and I knew we didn't have much time before the warlocks started their ritual.

Above us the canopy of the great ash tree, *Yggdrasil*, shivered in the breeze. Some leaves fluttered down, and I wondered if Lasinta had somehow damaged her with the spell she'd cast. I went up to sniff the bark, searching for any sign of charring.

"Oh don't worry, Dragoncat," the Oracle Fairy said. "It will take a lot more than a bolt of lightning to harm me."

"That's something," I said. "What's happened to Queen Ca'mun?"

"She had other things to be getting on with – a whole

kingdom to manage – but rest assured, she's aiding us in whatever way she can."

Max strolled over and crouched down beneath the Oracle Fairy's face on the tree bole. His tail thumped against the ground. He spoke to her in the dog language – this time in a succession of whines.

"You should have heard what Lasinta threatened to do. She's going to take control of all the dragons. Oh, Corralsa, I wish I could talk to you right now. I wish I could warn you."

Corralsa was Max's dragon, and before that she'd been bonded to the Warlock Prince, Arran. But Arran had treated both Max and Corralsa very badly, and so I guess they'd formed a friendship which had ended with dog and dragon bonding with each other. Corralsa was the only jet-black dragon I knew, her scales as shiny as gemstones. She was also almost as large as Aleam's great white, Olan, and so I didn't doubt that she'd also be a target in the warlocks' plans.

"Lasinta will be no threat to me if you stop her," the Oracle Fairy replied, and now she spoke in the human language, for Asinda and Seramina had reached the clifftop, having left Shadorow to sleep on the beach below. "But indeed, what she said is worrying. I heard it all, as Brigit and I together kept watch over all of you in those dreams."

"So do you know the ritual they spoke of?" Seramina asked as she strolled up to the giant ash tree. "The warlocks called it the Ritual of Arcanas, but I don't recall it from any of my books."

I could swear that the Oracle Fairy shuddered as it heard the name of the ritual, and more giant leaves fell from great heights. A squirrel emerged on a lower branch and chittered as if complaining about being woken up. From somewhere nearby, I smelled resin forming.

"I do not know how Lasinta heard of it," the Oracle Fairy said, "but I did see it once, a long time ago – through different roots in a different realm. The Pharaoh Warlocks tried such a thing to convert the dragons to their cause.

"It requires a crystal that joins other crystals together. A crystal like your Great Crystal in Dragonsbond Academy, to which all of your crystals are connected. The ritual involves leaching all the regular magic out of the crystal, to be replaced by dark magic – *Cana Dei*. Simultaneously, the same change occurs in all connected crystals, starting with the crystal of a certain white host dragon. Eventually, as the darkness seeps through from crystal to crystal, it affects the bonds between riders and dragons, and eventually creeps into their minds. Every pair has the chance to resist, but that would mean the breaking of their crystal. The choice is to submit or to die."

Asinda and Seramina looked at each other, and I heard them both suck in a breath. I also felt my heart skip a few beats; there was a reason that they had chosen Dragonsbond Academy as the target. Regular dragon riders might sacrifice themselves to save the world, but I couldn't imagine any of the young students doing this. Salanraja had warned me about what would happen if someone destroyed the crystal in her chamber – that we wouldn't survive it. They say it wouldn't just break our bond, but also break the spine of our souls in two.

A red admiral butterfly landed on a nearby flower and Max lowered himself to the grass, ready to stalk it.

"Concentrate, Max," I said. Really, when it came to this dog I sometimes felt like a schoolteacher. "Now you've got the gift of all languages, I know that you can understand all this."

"But the crystal also gave me the gift of multitasking," Max said. "I can do as many things as I like."

"Really? So how many gifts did it give you, then?" I asked.

"Just three," Max barked back. "You get three and I get three. It seems fair."

I knew Max's third ability – he couldn't be harmed by any magic. Though admittedly I hadn't seen him use that one for a long, long time. Presently, the Sussex spaniel leaped at the butterfly, and surprisingly he caught it in his forepaws. He shook it around for a minute and then let it go. The butterfly looked awfully happy to get away.

"When you're quite finished, Dragoncat," the Oracle Fairy said, the eyes within the two great whorls that formed their sockets looking down upon me.

"But Max caused the disturbance."

"Just shut up, Ben," Esme said. "Let the dog be a dog."

"Fine." I looked up at the Oracle Fairy. "You may continue."

"Yes," the Oracle Fairy said, and the canopy above us shivered once more, letting down a fresh flurry of leaves. It made me wonder if the giant ash tree had a cold. "Now, where was I?"

"The Great Crystal," Seramina said. "Please don't tell me the warlocks have it."

"I'm afraid they do," the Oracle Fairy replied. "They used the fairies to bring Dragonsbond Academy over here – an independent castle in the middle of the countryside, it contained the easiest of the large crystals for them to steal. And now they have it in the Faerie Realm, they can readily perform the Rite of Arcanas."

"But the Great Crystal was in place just before we left," I said. "How did they manage to get it out of there?"

"Using an awful lot of fairies … they took advantage of the time you spent in the dream world. Queen Ca'mun visited during that time, only to discover the crystal had completely vanished from its place in your castle courtyard."

"Whiskers," I said. "They moved fast."

"Indeed they did," the Oracle Fairy said. "Much faster

than I'd imagined they could. But then, you know how bad I am with time."

"So how long do *we* have, exactly?" Asinda asked.

"If they perform the ritual correctly, you will have until the top edge of the sun is swallowed by the horizon and the top edge of the moon emerges. At that point, they will have control of the dragons, and then there will be no turning back."

"And when exactly does the sun set?" Esme asked.

"Oh, it's ... you know, it's difficult to understand your interpretation of time for a creature like me who lives in Deep Time. I ... I think for you, a couple of hours. Three, tops."

"Whiskers," I said. "We have to move now."

"Indeed, you do ... I will send you back to Dragonsbond Academy, where Queen Ca'mun and her fairies are busy removing the last traces of the spell cast upon the castle."

We didn't have a moment to argue, because the Oracle Fairy blinked and this time the whole forest seemed to shiver, including the blades of grass underfoot. Another flash of white light, and there came a coolness, followed by a blast of heat.

Then we were back on the cobblestones in Dragonsbond Academy's bailey, and it was like we hadn't left at all.

34

COLLECTIVE IMPUDENCE

By the time we'd arrived back in Dragonsbond Academy, the sun had gained its first hint of sunset red, and a few clouds had appeared in the sky. If I looked at any one of them long enough, I could swear they were fringed with purple, but surely it had to be my imagination.

As before, the bailey and the inner courtyard remained deserted, empty of students and teachers. Not even the cats had been let out of the cattery to stalk mice – but I guess to have done that in the Faerie Realm might cause a diplomatic incident. If they started hunting Ca'mun's fairies, that were darting around everywhere in the academy, we might end up with a whole host of beetles to perform rat catching duties instead of cats.

The fairies moved like shiny flies, darting down to the ground, and then sweeping back up. They moved swiftly, and I guessed they were cleaning up any remnants of fairy dust. Still, I could smell honey in the air.

As soon as I saw Ca'mun emerge into the bailey of Dragonsbond Academy, her red cloak whipping out behind her and her soft cheeks seeming to glow, I began to worry about Ta'ra again.

Through all this travelling in the dream world I'd forgotten about her, but like the rest of the fairies in Faerini she'd be under Lasinta's control.

I just hoped she was okay, that she would somehow survive through this and decide that Ta'lon and the Faerie Realm wasn't the right place for her. Maybe Rine was right; maybe I could have two *companions*. It would be like in the Alhambra – the old Ragamuffin had told us how, in the great palace's gardens, cats would often have many more than two. I was sure Esme wouldn't mind, although I couldn't say the same for Ta'ra.

Before Ca'mun even spoke to us, she looked up at Asinda's charcoal dragon, Shadorow, towering above her. The fairy queen's eyes glazed with contempt, and she waved the dragon off.

"Get it away from me," she said. "Those filthy creatures should never be allowed anywhere near fairies. It's an insult to our kind."

Asinda shook her head and gave Ca'mun an acerbic look. But before she could even say anything, Seramina leaned over to whisper in Asinda's ear. Asinda tightened her jaw and shook her head, saying nothing.

With an angry grunt, Shadorow lifted up into the air and flew in the direction of the East Tower – although from the position of the sun I guessed it was now more like north. Shadorow's chamber in Dragonsbond Academy used to be right under Salanraja's, and no dragons had occupied it since.

Ca'mun watched Shadorow go, brushing herself off with her hands as if cleaning herself of dog hairs. She turned to Seramina.

"Our work here is almost done," she said, her voice too

high pitched for my sensitive ears to appreciate. "We have posted fairies in each dormitory to remove any memory loss or mental glamours from the minds of your students. We're also casting spells to remove the tiredness that Faerini's fairies had enchanted upon this castle. It seems that the warlocks wanted them to dream. More fairies are removing the spells from your dragons as I speak. It's a grand operation, I tell you, and we will visit Illumine Kingdom to discuss a fitting tribute from King Garmin once this is over."

Asinda scoffed. "Indeed," she said. "I've heard fairies never do anything for free. I just hope Lasinta's idiocy doesn't end up landing our country in irrecoverable debt."

Ca'mun turned her head towards Asinda. Their gazes met like steel clashing against steel.

"And who, pray tell are you?" the fairy queen asked.

"Driar Asinda," she replied. "I'm second removed from the royal line, and also a full-fledged member of the king's Dragon Guard. Naturally, I know King Garmin well."

She didn't add that she'd only just graduated from Dragonsbond Academy, but I guess the fairies didn't need to know that.

"Perhaps you can serve as an envoy for your king," Ca'mun said. "Don't worry, there will be no need for negotiations. I have already decided on Feyliyane Kingdom's terms."

Fortunately no one added that the elderly warlock Lasinta was also part of the royal line. Asinda was in fact her grand-niece, which is why the red-haired young woman could use dark magic. I had no idea where Esme and I had got our affinity for dark magic, though – perhaps it was a cat thing.

A golden fairy wisp buzzed close to Ca'mun's ear. She tilted her head, then nodded curtly.

"Right, it is done," she said. "You may communicate with your dragons now."

She clicked her fingers. Salanraja's voice immediately chimed in my mind.

"*Bengie?*" she asked.

"*Salanraja! Finally—*"

"*Have you been blocking me out again? Because I told you what would happen if you did. Wait, please don't tell me this has something to do with* Cana Dei. *You know how dangerous that stuff is, Bengie.*"

Whiskers, she could be so stupid sometimes.

"*I heard that,*" Salanraja said.

"*Salanraja … you're impossible. Of course I didn't block you out,*" I said. "*Just talk to the other dragons. King So'ta's fairies sprayed a pile of fairy dust around the academy, which damaged the connection between riders and dragons and affected everyone's memory. Now, Queen Ca'mun …*"

I continued to tell Salanraja everything. It seemed the fairy dust had sapped some of her memory away; she remembered little about our encounter with Ta'ra, Lasinta, Ta'lon and So'ta in the glade, so I had to fill her in on the details.

After that, it must have taken Esme, Seramina, Asinda and me a good half an hour – while the sun burned its descent through the sky – to explain to the rest of Dragonsbond Academy what had happened.

At their dragons' request, the Council of Three called Esme, Seramina, Asinda and me to the Council Chamber. The fairy dust had also managed to seep its way into the room during our absence, so the three elders were also half-clueless and needing to be filled in on much of what had happened.

Next they called an assembly in the central courtyard. Impressively, it filled up with students incredibly quickly, everyone muttering amongst themselves and causing a racket. This time none of the Council of Three had the strength to quiet them down, despite Driar Yila screaming at the top of her voice as usual. It appeared that the Initiates were finding it hard to take the meeting seriously with the absence of the Great Crystal; they all seemed to think this conclave was a joke.

It took a lot of convincing for any of them to even latch onto the idea that we were actually in the Faerie Realm, and even then most students didn't get it.

As I stood there in the crowd, golden wisps darted around us. One came really close to my face, and I instinctively raised my paw to bat it away before I realised what I was doing. The fairy was far too small for me to see its face, but it buzzed its wings faster as it flew away as if to admonish me. I guessed the fairy would complain to Ca'mun, who would in turn add a hefty amount to King Garmin's 'tribute'.

Meanwhile, rumours arose amongst the students that this had to be another test – I heard it all as I dashed around the legs of the students, taking in smells of disbelief, adrenaline, and mischief suffusing the courtyard. It would have been much easier for the Council of Three to convince them had the teachers believed us. But they also behaved as if this were some kind of elaborate prank. It was as if So'ta's fairy magic had permanently rewired the brains of everyone here, save for a select few of us.

"*Stupid humans,*" Salanraja said. "*Their brains are so brittle. Once they've set their mind on something, it's hard to get them to accept the greater truth.*"

"*So the dragons aren't having as hard a time believing?*"

"*No ... the dragons have pretty much worked out what's going on.*"

That was something, I guess. If the warlocks were going to work on the dragons first, then we needed them on our side.

Thus, as the westering sun continued to redden, and the

sky took on a deeper shade of velvet blue, I worried that the worst was to come. We wouldn't be able to muster a large enough force to stop the warlocks' schemes. The sun would set, the warlocks would complete the Ritual of Arcanas, and we would be the first dragons and riders to join their army – bound in servitude to Lasinta herself.

Eventually, Driar Yila gave in and dismissed the assembly. As she spoke, Driar Brigel moved to the back of the dais to talk to Driar Aleam.

"Be off with you, then," Driar Yila said. "I will deal with this impudence later. I am incredibly disappointed in you all."

Giggles arose amongst the assembly – I think they must have inherited some of the fairy mischief from the specks of fairy dust lodged in their brains. For a moment I wondered if Seramina, Esme, Max, Asinda and I would fight Lasinta and the warlocks alone. We'd probably at least be able to bring our dragons. But not even a thousand dragons would stand a chance against six warlocks and the whole host of magical creatures they were bound to have summoned to do their bidding.

In addition, we had hypnotised fairies to deal with. I really hoped I wouldn't have to go up against Ta'ra.

The crowd filtered out quickly, apparently happy to get away from the courtyard and back indoors. If anything, they seemed to have enjoyed the time off from their studies. Most of the teachers also departed through the double doors of the Keep Tower. Out of all of them, only Aleam and the Council of Three stayed put.

"By the way, the following students are to stay," Driar Yila continued. "Prefect Rine, Prefect Ange, Initiate Esme, Initiate Ben, Initiate Max, Prefect Kamino, and High Prefect Bellari. Oh, and Driar Asinda, if you could please join us too. We'll need you for a mission of utmost importance."

"Did she say High Prefect Bellari?" I asked Esme, who sat between Seramina's legs, grooming her fur.

"I think so," Esme said. "Yes, definitely High Prefect."

"Whiskers ... what is happening to these people?"

Really, I wondered if the Council of Three had lost their minds.

35

WHAT HAPPENS IN LA-LA LAND ...

The amber sun dipped beneath the wall of the Dragonsbond Academy courtyard; from its hiding place it stretched its rays over a thickening and deepening layer of cloud. I'd never seen it rain in the Faerie Realm, but then I knew it had to rain here sometimes. After all, the fairies needed to get their water from somewhere. Like the mutton sausage in Rine's dream, you could consume glamoured water, but it wouldn't do much for you biologically.

There came a distant rumble of thunder, although I saw no lightning. The air was charged with particles, and a cool wind picked up from the direction of the clouds.

All the students had left the courtyard by now, along with most of the teachers. Only Driar Aleam, and the elders of the Council of Three remained at the front.

The blonde-haired Bellari and her burly-shouldered boyfriend, Kamino, stood at the foot of the dais, both of them staring up at the elders as if they'd suddenly decided to become model students. She wore a red cloak, and she already had on the yellow pauldrons that denoted her position as a prefect. He wore no cloak at all, only a grey vest, and he'd positioned his prefect's pauldrons so high at the shoulders that he clearly wanted to show everyone his muscles. His staff on his back had a white crystal in it, which meant he was probably a shield mage.

Ange walked up to stand beside Bellari. She also wore her yellow prefect pauldrons, and this time a green cloak. Pali-mali, Ange's cheetah, followed her. She kept her distance from Bellari though.

I made a mental note to tell the desert cheetah later that it was a good idea to annoy Bellari as much as possible. Our new 'High Prefect' deserved all the sneezes we animals could give her. Plus, she might order Kamino to kick us small cats, but I'd like to see him daring to kick a desert cheetah.

I turned my ears to hear Ange say, "So, High Prefect. Congratulations, Bellari ... I mean it."

Bellari had her back turned towards me, but I could all but imagine the gloating look on her face as she turned to Ange. Those two had once been good friends, but Bellari seemed to think Ange had stolen Rine from her. In all honesty, I guess she had – and I had helped her do it. I was rather proud of that.

Now in a perfect world I would have thought Ange would assume Lars' former role of High Prefect – the most senior role among the students. Ange was after all hard-working, studious, and an incredibly adept leaf mage.

I went up to Rine, who was standing next to Seramina and watching the exchange between his girlfriend and ex-girlfriend with interest.

"How did Bellari get to be High Prefect?" I asked him. "And how come you knew about it? I was there in your dream when you mentioned she would be appointed. And then it went ahead and happened."

Rine glanced at Seramina. "You were in my dream? Wait a minute ... you saw all that? I thought it seemed strange how you were all sitting over on the other side of the fire talking amongst yourselves."

Seramina nodded. "Ben had his first experience of dreamwalking, aided by the Oracle Fairy. It was how we learned exactly what was going on."

"Well," Rine said. "All I can say is that we were all very sleepy, and I think I did a lot of dreaming. Shame I had to wake up, really. It was a good dream."

"No it wasn't," I said. "It was a horrible dream! Ange is your girlfriend, not Bellari."

Rine snorted. "It was only a dream, Ben. And what happens in la-la land stays in la-la land, if you know what I mean."

"It's just that you seem proud of it," I said.

"Well ..." Rine said, and he dropped his voice to the level of a conspiratorial whisper, "as I said, it was a good dream."

"No – it – wasn't!"

"Was for me ... anyway, about Bellari being High Prefect. I wouldn't let it get to you; these things are all about money, and Bellari's grandmother on her late mother's side has given a lot to the school."

"So what you're telling me is that Bellari's family bought her position as High Prefect? And no doubt you're saying the same of Lars?"

"That's the way of things, Ben," Rine said with a shrug. "Schools need funding, and they have to give their investors something in return. Anyway, I think we have bigger things to worry about."

He then turned towards the dais that Aleam, Asinda, and the Council of Three were standing on, talking amongst themselves. Now that Asinda was a fully graduated dragon rider, she had the authority to stand up there without the Council of Three's permission. Yet the way she kept her head slightly lowered as she spoke to them made it obvious who was actually in charge.

Still, I could hear fairies flying around everywhere as they performed all necessary clean-up tasks around the castle. The way that their wings buzzed made them sound like bees on helium.

I'd learned from my eavesdropping on the conversations on the dais that Ca'mun had sent her fairies out before to find out which students and teachers weren't showing any aftereffects of the fairy dust. That was why the fairy had flown so awfully close to my face before – it was looking in my eyes for traces of gold, a sign that I wasn't fully in command of my faculties.

It turned out that only those present in the courtyard were safe to fly out against the warlocks without any risk of losing ourselves during the battle. If any of the other students came it would only take a flick of King So'ta's fingers to get them to turn and attack their friends.

Thus our forces were limited to only four human students, two cats, a dog, and two Driars – namely Asinda and Aleam. The Council of Three wasn't going to fly with us because they needed to stay and look after the academy just in case any students addled by the fairy dust tried anything.

In the empty space beneath where the crystal had once stood, a golden plume appeared. The air took on the scents of lavender and oleander, before Ca'mun's glamoured human form appeared. Her red cloak almost seemed to be shining now, its complex fairy weaves reflecting the red light coming off the thickening clouds.

Ca'mun didn't waste a second. "We have little time left —" she looked up at the sky as if to communicate that she was addressing everyone, "—perhaps an hour if that. The time for action is nigh."

Esme had positioned herself in front of the stage, not far

from Bellari and Kamino, but I guess far enough that she didn't affect our High Prefect's 'allergies'.

The Abyssinian seemed to have little patience for waiting around.

"So let's get on with it," she said, "because you fairies seem to have been wasting an awful lot of time."

Ca'mun looked down at Esme and narrowed her eyes. The way she was glaring, I half expected the fairy queen to click her fingers and turn Esme into whiskers-knows-what.

"You dare address a high royal of the fairy line in such a manner? I still don't know who you think you are."

"A daughter of Bastet," Esme said. "Which makes me like a princess."

"And I'm a queen."

I thought I'd go over and give Esme some emotional support. I rubbed my cheek against her side.

"We have an hour, do we not?" I asked. "So why does it matter who is queen or who is princess? We just need to get out there."

"Isn't it your academy that is under threat? They are performing the Ritual of Arcanas on you and not on us."

"You'll be next," I said. "Once they've controlled our dragons, the warlocks will have them rain fire on your cities and farms."

"Or Lasinta will find a way to control your precious kingdom of Feyliyane," Esme added. "Like they have with Faerini. They will no longer be your subjects, but follow the warlocks. How would you like that?"

Ca'mun's hand was raised up to the side of her body, her fingers poised. "I really don't like the tone you're taking with me. In all my life serving as a queen of the fairies, I've never encountered creatures so disrespectful."

Aleam stepped forwards from his position beside the

Council of Three. He shifted his brown robe, and then leaned on his staff for support.

"Now, now, Queen Ca'mun. You might find our feline Initiates here a little argumentative, but you know they are right. The question we've been discussing amongst ourselves is what aid will you provide? Because by our calculations and the limited cartographic records we have on the Faerie Realm in our library, it appears to be around ninety minutes' flight to the Aisean Wetlands."

Queen Ca'mun raised her head. The dimming light seemed to highlight the thin nostrils on her snub nose. "I will aid you, if these two creatures – these felines – apologise."

I turned to Esme. "Sensitive one, isn't she?" I said.

"Ben," Aleam said.

"*Listen to Aleam,*" Salanraja said in my mind. "*Because if you cause trouble with that fairy queen, you've doomed us all.*"

My tummy rumbled, and all I wanted to do was rush over to Asinda and beg for some of those thin chewy strips of beef.

"Fine," I said. "I'm sorry for almost causing a diplomatic incident, your great fairy highness."

I lowered myself on my front paws for a brief moment to imitate a human bow in the best way I could.

"*Potential* diplomatic incident," Ca'mun corrected.

"Potential diplomatic incident," I repeated. I also preferred the sound of that.

"Hmmph," Ca'mun said. My apology seemed to be acceptable to her, even though I'd laced it with sarcasm and irony. "And the white one? What do you have to say for yourself?"

"Don't you dare reduce me just to a colour," Esme said. "I'm an Abyssinian, the most beautiful breed of cat there is."

"You won't be for long if you don't say sorry," I said to her, my gaze completely focused on the fairy queen's trembling fingers.

"Fine," Esme said. "Sorry."

"Is that it?" Ca'mun asked.

"That's it," Esme said. "It's a very simple word, isn't it?"

Ca'mun sighed. She clicked her fingers, and a shiver ran down my spine as sparks jumped off from them. But nothing happened. Esme remained an Abyssinian, and I remained a Bengal.

"Then that will have to do. I will send enough of my people to battle any fairies we may encounter from Faerini. Their magic can speed up your journey time to twenty minutes, but any battle against the warlocks must be fought by humans and dragons alone."

"That will be sufficient," Aleam said, and he sketched a bow in spite of his creaking joints. "I thank you, your highness."

"Very well," Ca'mun said. "I will ready my fairies. Can you gather your forces and leave in ten minutes?"

Aleam nodded, then he clapped his hands and relayed the information to everyone.

Ten minutes ... that would give me enough time to seek out Asinda and ask her for some more beef jerky. After all, I didn't want to be flying out to battle on an empty stomach.

36

FLIGHT OVER FAIRYLAND

Because I was an agile Bengal, a descendant of the great Asian leopard cat and the mighty George, I was first to reach my dragon in her chamber. Salanraja had already positioned herself in front of the opening, the sun falling towards the horizon on our left-hand side.

The ruby dragon turned her tail towards me to allow me a passage up, and I clambered to my usual position on her back. She took a running jump, leapt off into a slight dive, and spread her massive wings, entering a gentle glide.

Wind swept through her corridor of spikes. The sun had now reached a level where I could watch the speed of its path if I focused on it. We really didn't have long left.

The other dragons weren't far behind us. Next came Gratis – Esme's jet-black dwarf dragon, like Corralsa except much, much smaller. Speaking of Corralsa, she followed after with Max on top of her, seeming to displace the air with her massive bulk. An emerald and a sapphire dragon followed. These were Ishtkar, Rine's dragon, and Quarl, Ange's dragon. Both young dragon riders sat right at the crook of their dragon's necks, their staffs moving as they swayed in flight.

The two charcoals followed – Shadorow and Hallinar, Asinda's and Seramina's dragons respectively. Then came two citrines, Pinacole with Bellari riding, and I didn't know the name of Kamino's dragon.

As usual in such flights, Aleam's great white dragon, Olan, came out last, but her launch was so powerful that the other dragons swept out of the way for her. She was the strongest flier, apart from Corralsa, and so she took the head of the formation. The rest of us grouped ourselves on to the wings of a V with Shadorow on one end and Hallinar on the other. Olan's great pinions swept the path for us, providing a good boost to our speed without any need for magic.

Then came the fairies, swarming out from the bailey like bees from a hive. I only noticed them when there were enough of them upon us. They spun a tight cocoon around our formation, and Hallinar and Seramina pulled in the edges of the V to enter their embrace. The fairies therefore formed a tunnel around us that sped us all up, carrying us upon currents of wind buffed by the fairy dust.

We travelled a long way in this manner, and we saw quite a lot.

We passed brilliant turquoise lakes, and forests as green as limes. We flew over fields of flowers of every possible colour, and great grassy plains with limestone boulders that stuck out like stubble. We saw worn karst landscapes, and tall mountain peaks, and towering glaciers. We also saw braided streams, and foaming waterfalls, and alluvial fans of dried sediment that spilled into sweeping valleys. The beauty of the Faerie Realm was immense, and I would have never thought we were travelling towards a battle.

These could have been the very last things I saw, but at least I'd lived to see them. Oh, the stories I could have told the old Ragamuffin if he knew me today.

Salanraja also seemed to be basking in appreciation.

"Never in my life would I have expected to see so much of the Faerie Realm," she said. *"These were tales that only Bestian told, in his famous academy. Now I'm seeing it for myself. Maybe when you're done, I'll also be teaching dragons like Bestian is now, and telling such great tales."*

"What do you mean, when I'm done?" I asked.

"Well, I'm a dragon and you're a cat. That means I'll most likely live a lot longer than you will."

"I thought that life becomes unbearable once the bond between a dragon and her rider is severed."

"Indeed," Salanraja said. *"The keyword there is 'severed'. But if a dragon rider dies of old age, then the dragon grieves for a while and afterwards gets to enjoy a retirement. Matharon chose to delay his retirement so that he could teach dragons how to better align with humans – and I guess that includes other animals now too."*

"Retirement?" I said. *"Our retirement is meant to be in a country cottage with Rine and Ange and Esme. Seramina can join us if she wishes, and perhaps Ta'ra will one day too, once she's done with her silliness in the Faerie Realm. But it will be a no-Bellari zone. We'll put a sign up on the door, and if I ever catch Rine dreaming about her again – even if he mutters her name in his sleep – I'll scratch his leg.*

"You dragons can stay in a big field around the back, and we'll require three villages, with all kinds of livestock farms, to support you. But that's okay, because we'll all be so famous by then and have so much money that we can employ anyone we need. They can bring you the best food, and you can roast it in the special way that you have. It will be wonderful, Salanraja. We'll have the best retirement possible."

"So you keep telling me," Salanraja said. *"But I mean after that – when I really retire. Because it sounds like your version of retirement will be a full-time job for me."*

I growled, but said nothing. Talking about this – just

dreaming about my future – had made me forget that we were flying into battle. Admittedly, if the warlocks got their way, none of this would come to pass.

I spent the rest of the journey watching the heavy clouds continue to develop above Dragonsbond Academy. A thick grey layer of rain streaked down over the castle, almost concealing it from view. We had managed to get ahead of the storm, but now I could see it was gaining on us.

While I felt the rush of the wind from in front due to our flight, an even stronger wind seemed to buffet us from behind. One seemed to follow the other, like waves that tossed Salanraja up and down in the sky.

Though I'd flown enough on dragonback to say I was used to flying, I'd still never encountered conditions like this. It took all my focus not to throw up on Salanraja's back – she'd hated it whenever I'd done that. It seemed that we wouldn't only have to battle the warlocks, but also the weather. Why, when the worst things happened, did they always have to occur in the rain?

Still, the sun remained ahead of us, and we flew steadily towards its amber glare. It let off a little heat that warded off the chill wind, but that heat was slowly dissipating.

Across the horizon, I thought I could make out a faint streak of white. Could that be the moon getting ready to rise? But it had to be my imagination – surely it wouldn't be bright enough.

All of a sudden, there was a roar from up ahead; Olan had spotted something. Together, the rest of the dragons bellowed a response.

By this point we had reached a far wetter land. Damp reeds stuck out of the swamps below us, and the marshes themselves spawned a natural cover of mist, with a purple taint spreading through it. Herons and other aquatic birds dabbled their long beaks into the water for fish.

Where the mist didn't fall the sun cast brilliant magmatic displays over the patches of water. As the lakes rippled, the reflections danced, making it look as if the whole place was on fire.

In the distance, a white pinprick of light shone even brighter than the sun. That must have been the grand crystal I saw, with purple mist swarming up around it. The warlocks were close.

But our focus wasn't on them.

Instead, I squinted my eyes and saw a dragon hovering above the quickly descending sun. It was a white dwarf dragon, and I recognised it as Kada.

It didn't take me long to see his rider, the black cat and my former *companion* Ta'ra, sitting casually on his head.

37

PRISONER À LA
SCHRÖDINGER'S CAT

The sun had almost touched the horizon, sending out brilliant beams of red that highlighted the dwarf dragon, Kada's, underbelly. Ta'ra still sat on the dragon's head, looking over at us. A gust of wind came to us from the west, carrying upon it the honey-scent of fairy dust, and the even fainter stench of rotten vegetable juice.

Olan stopped, hovering in front of the pair, and the rest of the dragons including Salanraja gathered in a semicircle. Around Ta'ra the occasional golden glint caught the light, and I knew that she had fairies accompanying her.

In front of us, our own fairies gathered in a swarm. They fanned out to create a glistening wall between us and Ta'ra, just in case she had any tricks up her sleeve. She wouldn't – she was just a normal cat, now – but the fairies accompanying her might.

Under normal conditions, Ta'ra should have been much too far away for us to hear her. Especially with the wind now screaming up from behind us, signalling the accelerating storm. But she had fairy magic on her side, and so her voice boomed out over the sky.

She spoke in the human language: "Lasinta and the warlocks send their regards, and I've been sent forth as a messenger."

I wondered who out of all of us had a voice loud enough to respond. Asinda perhaps could have tried, but she'd probably have lost her voice by the end of it. She didn't have to, though, because the shimmering wall of fairies and fairy dust at the front of our formation glistened brightly, and a faint humming sound emerged from the centre of the wall. Or at least it started off faint, because soon waves of light spread out across the wall and the sound intensified. Ca'mun's shrill voice emerged out of this, as loud as thunder in the absence of any rain.

"Princess Ta'ra of Faerini," she said. "You are a fairy no more. Your actions and Faerini's are severe enough to declare war on our kingdom, and I say that with a heavy heart knowing that the fairy kingdoms have not had to fight for hundreds of years. But alas, King So'ta must answer for his crimes."

Kada flapped his wings a couple of times to stay aloft. Together, the fairies on her side sent out some bright flashes of light, as if to express an anger of their own.

"King So'ta is no longer king of Faerini," Ta'ra bawled back. "The mantle of monarch has passed to the warlock Lasinta, and the warlocks Moonz, Pladana, Cala, Junas, and Ritrad are present at her court."

"Ridiculous," Ca'mun called back, the fairy wall in front of us flaring brightly. "A human cannot rule a fairy kingdom."

Ta'ra let out a cackle of laughter. Except it wasn't Ta'ra's feline voice now coming out of her mouth, but Lasinta's croaky warlock one. "Your realm is about to change, Ca'mun – and we've not yet decided whether your actions warrant your survival under our rule, or your destruction. Your behaviour today shall determine how that shall go."

"Such ridicule," Ca'mun said. "Such delusions of grandeur. There are six of you today, against a kingdom of fairies escorting a solid troop of dragons and riders. You do not stand a chance."

"Well, if you are to stop us, you'd better hurry. Because as you can see the sun has almost set, and once it does everything changes for you, my dear fairy queen."

The wall of fairies flashed again. Out of it boomed Ca'mun's voice, accompanied by a chilly gust of wind. "Impudence! Take the Cat Sidhe prisoner!"

Flashes shot across the wall as other high-pitched fairy voices echoed out from it: "Take her prisoner! Cat Sidhe Princess! Traitor! Prisoner! For Feyliyane!"

The hackles shot up on my fur, and I bristled as I heard the anger in their voices. What were they about to do to Ta'ra? They could kill her. If they did, everything that I'd fought for would become meaningless. I wanted her back in my life. I missed her ...

"Don't harm her!" I shouted, but my voice was lost in the wind carrying the gravid thunderclouds from behind. Still, I tried. "She's innocent!"

The wall of fairies gathered up into a sphere, which looked like a shiny ball of yarn with a trailing tail as it charged forward. The golden glows surrounding Ta'ra and Kada also gathered into a ball of their own, but the size of theirs was much smaller.

Soon, shrill screeches pierced the sky. Fairy war cries had to be the most terrifying sound I'd ever heard.

"No!" I screamed.

A roar of thunder responded from the sky.

The two balls of fairies clashed, and Ca'mun's swarm overwhelmed the other. Then they surrounded Ta'ra, and she was engulfed in a ball of white glowing anger, screeching and flashing away.

Presently Ca'mun's fairy swarm drifted down to the ground. Like the proverbial cat trapped in a quantum box, I couldn't tell if she was alive or dead.

# THE GREAT CRYSTAL

The swamp blazed with reflections of sun fire. Looking upon it was like looking into a thousand portals to the Seventh Dimension. Seramina's vision had looked just like this, when she had split the earth open and summoned the demons out of oblivion.

From behind me came a flash of lightning, then a boom of thunder. The clouds opened up and down came the buckets of rain, drenching my fur and trickling down Salanraja's scales underfoot. It seemed to wash away the fairies that surrounded Ta'ra.

Still, I had no idea if she was alive or dead.

"They wouldn't have killed her," Salanraja said. *"Not Queen Ca'mun ... not even she is that cruel."*

"You weren't there when she threatened to turn us all into beetles and feed us to the crows."

"Threat is different to action, Bengie ..."

"Ben."

"Fine ... Ben."

Meanwhile the sun teetered over the horizon, accelerating onwards. After it fell we would see the moon rise, and then the apocalypse would be nigh. It seemed to be fighting back the rain, which continued to fall over us in rivulets; even the clouds here seemed to be scared of the crimson sun, as if fully aware of the omen that it would bring.

Beneath us, the fairy swarm dissipated, and I saw Ta'ra lying on the ground, Kada right beside her. We were too far up to see if either of them was breathing.

"Is she alive? Salanraja, we need to fly down to see."

"We don't have time, Bengie. Come on, it's starting."

"But Ta'ra, she could be ..."

Salanraja was right, of course. If we didn't stop the warlocks' ritual, then I'd never find out if she'd survived. Lasinta would take control of Olan's mind, then Salanraja's, and then mine. Eventually *Cana Dei* would creep in, and I wouldn't care if I was alive or dead, let alone what had happened to Ta'ra.

As the sun continued its descent, a thin white beam shone up from where that tiny pinprick of white light had adorned the horizon. Together the dragons roared, and Salanraja bucked as they flew back into formation.

The fairies drifted upwards from the ground. They wrapped us in their spiralling cocoon once again, speeding us on much faster than we had travelled before.

The rain poured down, but we were going so fast that we seemed to be avoiding the drops. The swamps spun by below us. As if sensing the danger, the waterfowl rose up from their feeding grounds and flew away from the billowing clouds.

Together we charged towards a landscape redolent with rotten vegetable juice, flying low over the ground. Soon we found the Great Crystal hovering in the air and spinning on its longitudinal axis. It towered high above the six warlocks who had gathered around it, pumping purple magic into it from the beams coming out of their staffs.

Purple smoke billowed above the swamps, as if coming

out of the marshes themselves. The water surrounding the island bubbled violently, and I could smell pockets of sulphur amidst the stench of dark magic. This marsh was decaying, and fast.

"*It's terrible,*" I said to Salanraja, my jaw clenched. "*They're destroying this place.*"

"*That and the crystal,*" Salanraja said. "*If we lose any of these Great Crystals, then our destiny changes. We enter a future more uncertain than anyone has ever known.*"

The crystal itself glowed bright white, and the occasional purple spark flashed across its interior. In my head, I could hear very faint murmurs of an ancient language that even I couldn't understand. I knew the languages of every single living creature, but the crystals weren't alive.

One thing for sure, the voices were afraid, calling out for help to any mind that could hear them. But the crystal no longer had the ability to translate its fears into language; the warlocks were sapping all its power away.

A massive pile of inert demon rats traced over the ground around and below the crystal. They'd been arranged to look like a crater, or perhaps the downward force of the crystal's magic had pushed them outwards.

Whiskers, I might have known they were the demon rats that I'd seen Ta'ra hunting in the glade. Lasinta and the warlocks had summoned them here from the Seventh Dimension. Warlocks always seemed to use them for powerful magic – I had no idea why.

A thick red beam was shooting upwards from the centre of the crater. A faint red sheet of light spanned across the top of the valley. It formed the impression of a portal into a land of red rock and brimstone. If it gained enough strength, demons could swarm out of it and the fairies wouldn't stand a chance.

For now, the portal was strong enough to supply demon

magic from the Seventh Dimension, clearly contributing to the ritual. The demon snake Apopis must have had something to do with this. If not him, perhaps the lion-hippopotamus-crocodile demon queen, Ammit herself, was involved.

She commanded an army of demon hippopotamuses, and I wouldn't have been surprised to see them pile out of the crater.

The sun had become a huge semicircle on the horizon. Fortunately for us it seemed to set slower in the Faerie Realm. Still, we only had minutes before it disappeared and the moon rose ...

Suddenly, there came a chorus of screeches from the ground. Wispy manipulators formed from purple crystals strewn across it. They raised their staffs into the air to cast a host of bone dragons, all of them facing our convoy, red light glinting off their skeletal teeth.

One of them dived straight towards Salanraja and me. As it fell, its cry cut the air apart once again.

BRIMMING WITH POWER

From above the shimmering swamps, the glowing Great Crystal, the nearly complete Ritual of Arcanas, and the crater of demon rats, a bone dragon charged through the pouring rain.

Its purple glowing gaze bore down on us. It had no substance, only a ribcage as thick as a mammoth's covering a purple glowing core.

Its tail creaked as it swished it about. Out of its open mouth came a purple cloud of searing acid, close enough to burn me to dust.

Salanraja didn't stay to fight; rather she swooped down under its path, missing the acid by inches. But I breathed in a remnant of it, burning my throat so much that I would have a harsh meow for days.

My dragon dived towards a sun that had almost left the horizon. It had lost its comforting glow and would soon be replaced by a cold blue moon. As if to challenge her, the rain came down even harder, not just as shining drops but also icy sleet and hail.

It felt like passing through a melting waterfall, except this one seemed to extend to infinity, or at least to a threshold where the clouds tumbled into the sunset. Despite this onslaught of weather, the warlocks didn't cease their ritual, so I knew we couldn't give up the fight even with my fur drenched to the skin.

"You know the drill, Bengie," Salanraja said.

"Can't you at least use my proper name, just once? Particularly since this looks like the end."

"Just shut up and fight," she said. *"We still have time."*

I was sitting on her head, which she lowered to the ground as she dived towards it. Just inches from the reeds of the island, she spread out her wings, jerking herself to a halt.

I tumbled down off her nose and onto the ground. But I was ready for it, and I rolled through the reeds.

I did two things at once: First, I willed myself to turn into a chimera. My muscles popped and creaked, and the transformation swept over me quickly. My three heads roared and bleated and hissed into the open air.

I also summoned my staff bearer. The giant white hand plunged my staff into the mouth of my lion's head. I revelled in the warmth at the back of my rough tongue. I rejoiced in the power surging through every inch of my body.

Dark magic – I had no choice. It was the only way to win.

Through the colourful thermal vision of my snake's eyes, I could now see the fairies. Golden glows danced around the hailstones, and I could see how they moved in pairs. Tiny sparks of magic flashed between each pair, and it didn't take me long to recognise how Ca'mun's and So'ta's forces were locked in battle. Without Ca'mun's escorts, the Faerini fairies would have overwhelmed us before we'd even had a chance to touch down.

The weather must also be a part of the warlocks' spell; they'd summoned powerful magic to keep Ca'mun's forces at bay. What better way to stop a swarm of fairies than with a cloud of hailstones?

Meanwhile, my human, feline, and canine comrades took up their positions around me. I didn't look at them, but focused on the manipulators who had turned their staffs towards us, cutting off the beams that they'd used to keep the bone dragons invincible.

I heard their shouts and yowls and barks. I saw their magic streaking across the landscape.

In the centre of them all, Kamino raised his staff. With a glow of pure white light, he set up a magical shield dome, and the rest of my fellow dragon riders gathered within it for protection. Sparks jumped off the blue shimmering dome surrounding them as the hail bounced away. Rine, Ange, Aleam, Seramina, Asinda, Esme and Max had all crowded together under his shield. Everyone except Max had their staffs ready.

They pushed forward like an elephant sweeping its way through a pack of hyenas. The manipulators shot streams of white magic at the dome, and my friends shot spells back. Crystals fell to the ground where icicles, fireballs, whipping vines, streaks of lightning, and bars of white magic had hit them at their spectral hearts.

I didn't dare join them – they were only a distraction. And at the pace they were going, there was no way they'd make it in time.

What really mattered was the six warlocks, who were completely focused on feeding their energy into the Great Crystal. More and more streaks of purple flashed beneath its facets. Closer and closer the crystal was coming to ending us all.

"*Go, Ben,*" Salanraja screamed in my mind. "*The sun has almost set. Only a chimera has the strength to power through.*"

"*I know,*" I said, and I clenched my jaws even tighter around my staff and charged.

The manipulators tried firing white beams at me, sharp enough to sear me in two. But I only batted them out of the way using the purple tendrils of magic from my staff. I was strong now ... I was invincible.

The manipulators tried another tactic. They summoned magical mandragoras out of the ground – great thorny plants with huge heads and sharp snapping jaws. Vines whipped at me as the heads lunged.

I took a few scratches, and I felt the poison trying to enter my bloodstream. But I had the dark magic, and I cast it over myself to keep safe.

The ground also erupted around me as fire and ice and lightning and vines and light flashed everywhere. My allies had noticed my charge and they had added their spells to support me. I could make it.

"*You're almost there,*" Salanraja said, and I caught a glimpse of her breathing fire over a bone dragon in my mind's eye, disintegrating it to ash.

"*And you're brimming with power,*" another voice said in my mind, deep and sonorous. The voice of *Cana Dei.* "*You will be among the first to turn to me, I think, Dragoncat. For now, continue the show.*"

I ignored that voice, or perhaps it filled me with even more power. I charged with the will of a warrior, flashing mighty magic around me as I went. This time, I was the leader – the mighty Dragoncat. I'd already defeated one warlock, and now I was going to defeat six others.

Suddenly I broke through the wall of rain and hail, my chimera and goat fur dripping. The warlocks were so focused on their task that I could strike any one of them down with a simple beam of dark magic.

Even a small interruption would be enough to break their ritual. That's all we needed.

Their eyes were glazed over and none of them seemed to notice my arrival. Probably they hadn't expected any of us to break through what they'd sent against us. Their arrogance would be their downfall.

I summoned all the power into my staff that I could. My eyes swam and my muscles burned with energy. Blood rushed to my cheeks and my head. I channelled every essence of my being into my staff.

"That's it, Dragoncat," said that voice again. *"Brimming with power…"*

The sun plunged beneath the horizon.

A brilliant beam of red destructive energy streamed out of my staff, heading straight for Lasinta.

The elderly warlock spun around, and an even brighter crimson beam met my own. Energy crashed against energy, and I was too weak.

I stumbled backwards and fell to the floor.

Lasinta's lips curled up in that wicked smile of hers. "You are too late, Dragoncat. The Ritual of Arcanas is complete."

Then the moon began to rise.

I watched it for a moment as it sailed up much quicker into the sky than the sun had set. The swamp waters no longer blazed with fire, but rather shone with silver.

Suddenly a pulse of purple light shot out of the Great Crystal. It flashed bright enough for me to see all the cracks within it. A wave of magic swept over my mind, so powerful that it washed all sensations away.

I could see, hear, smell, taste, and feel nothing.

Soon enough, the darkness closed in …

40

AN IMPOSSIBLE CHOICE

F lashes of darkness entered my vision, and the worlds as I knew them spun in circles. I saw cities of glass from the Fourth Dimension, and cities of stone in the First. I saw the bat-buzzard aeriosaurs flying through the dark sky of the Fifth Dimension; I saw Bastet with her golden torc shining as she gazed out across the River of Souls. I saw magma and brimstone, and great armies of every imaginable sort of demon creature looking up at their Demon Lord, Ammit. She was preparing for battle – was this all a part of the warlocks' plan?

I saw a muscular tabby with only one eye – my father the great and mighty George – stalking through the Ghost Realm and taking a drink from a fresh stream. Also in the Ghost Realm, I saw myself as a kitten against my mother's chest, cuddled up with all the other Bengals in her litter.

Then I saw Salanraja falling to the ground, bone dragons wheeling above her and no longer considering her a threat. She clawed at her scales as if wanting to tear herself apart. I felt each scratch, and I smelled fresh blood pouring out of her wounds.

"*Salanraja,*" I said. "*Salanraja, don't let her in.*"

"It's too late," she replied. *"Olan already taken ... must resist ... so beautiful ... I only need to follow the light."*

"No ... Salanraja. You must fight this. You can't lose control."

"It's too late, Bengie ... Ben ... Dragoncat ... it's too late."

I felt her slip away from me, and I'd expected it to feel like being severed in two. But rather it just felt as if my heart was empty; I had no reason to want to live any more.

The blackness returned, so stark that I couldn't even see patterns of light within it.

I'd had moments like this before, where I could only see darkness; moments where it had felt like all was lost. Since my earliest visit to the First Dimension, my crystal had always appeared in my visions and called me Dragoncat and told me exactly what to do next. It had always been there to pluck me out of the darkness, and to guide me through the deepest labyrinths of my subconscious.

But my crystal was no longer with me. As my bond with Salanraja had broken, so had my bond with my crystal.

Eventually, after I'd wallowed long enough in despair and blackness, I did see a light. It wasn't soft and warming, but evil and purple. It belonged to a giant sphere, hovering just in front of my nose. It pulsed brightly as Lasinta's voice emanated from it.

"Submit!" she commanded. "Submit, or die."

The sphere turned momentarily into her face, her cruel eyes looking down. She wasn't just looking at me, but across the minds of all her subjects. Now her army of dragons had to choose if they would bend to her will.

"I cannot submit," Salanraja said in my mind. *"I must choose the other path."*

"Salanraja, no!" I said. *"There has to be another way."*

"Another way ... oh, the light ... so beautiful ... follow the

light ... lead me to my heart's desires. But another way. The other way ... must not submit. Must choose death."

"Salanraja ..."

Her voice cut out in my mind again. Lasinta's face had once again become a sphere.

"Submit!"

"No!" I shouted back.

"Submit or die!"

Whiskers, it was futile. We were all doomed.

"Of course, you have a third option," a voice boomed out from behind me, deep and sonorous. I spun around to see another ball, this time one of darkness fringed with tiny balls of white light darting into and out of it like geysers.

"Lasinta is tightroping the precipice, while I am what dwells at the base of the abyss," *Cana Dei* said. "Join me, and we can end her. This can be over very quickly, if you would only embrace ..."

"No!" I replied. "No, you are even worse."

"'Better' and 'worse' only exist on a certain plane, Dragoncat. If you expand your mind to examine all the possibilities, you will see this way will favour us all in the best possible manner."

I felt a pull towards it, as if someone had wrapped a rope around my heart and was tugging on it gently. I was tempted, admittedly. All this pain, all this anguish. All I had to do was relax and let *Cana Dei* do the rest. It would guide me through the darkness.

"Submit!" Lasinta screamed out again from behind me. The earth rumbled underfoot. "Submit or die!"

"I will choose death," Salanraja said. *"That's the only choice ... but the light ... so beautiful ... if I could only live."*

"You need to make a choice, Dragoncat," *Cana Dei* said. "But know if you choose the warlock, I will find my way into your mind eventually. She can't hold me off forever – she's already playing a very dangerous game."

I really didn't know what to do. I think Salanraja was right; I had no choice but to die. But I couldn't let either the warlock or *Cana Dei* in.

Suddenly, something wet and warm splashed against my face. Then, I heard another voice in the darkness, even louder than the others. It barked like a dog. That's because it *was* a dog ...

"Wake up, Ben," Max said. "There's wargs! Wargs! Too many evil purple wargs!"

I heard other voices too. They belonged to the warlocks.

"How did the dog get through?"

"Not just him, look, the teenagers too."

"And that mangy cat. The white one. Stupid creature ..."

"To battle! We can't let them stop Lasinta."

Max licked my face for a second time. His breath stank horribly, it was disgusting. But I felt myself waking up.

"Wake up Ben!" Max barked again. "We need to fight. My crystal gave me a mission – you need to fight the wargs!"

Then Lasinta shouted again, "Submit! Submit or die!"

But I wasn't going to do either; and neither was I going to surrender myself to *Cana Dei*.

Instead I opened my eyes and picked myself up off the ground.

41

RETURN OF THE GUARDIANS

The Great Crystal loomed above me, glowing purple. It emitted a wide beam directed straight towards Lasinta, who sat with her legs crossed, levitating and surrounded by a mantle of glowing purple clouds.

Her eyes were closed, and her lips were moving fast as though incanting a thousand spells. Meanwhile, here I was lying on the ground in my usual Bengal form. I must have transformed when I'd been passed out.

"Submit!" Lasinta screamed, and the crystal, the beam leading into her, and the cloud around her flared bright white, sending out a powerful blast of heat. "Submit or die!"

I stood up, my legs shaking, and scanned the terrain around me. The rain clouds had retreated, and the moon was carving its upwards path through the midnight blue.

Rine, Ange, Bellari, Kamino and all our dragons lay sprawling on the ground behind me. They weren't the only dragons here though – every dragon lay across the ground, somehow having been magically transported here.

Across the island, rolling into the swamp, I could see scales of red, green, blue, yellow, white, and black shimmering as if part of a sea. They were also writhing on the ground, trying to battle Lasinta's attempts to take control. Whiskers, I hoped none of them decided to give up.

No fairies were anywhere to be seen. I guess Lasinta didn't need them anymore.

Nearly everything stank of rotten vegetable juice, but I could also smell my companions nearby. Snowdrop perfume, Asinda's jasmine scent, Max's canine stench, and Esme's sweet smell of catness.

We had all now awoken. Bastet's Guardians of the White and one Sussex spaniel – we stood up together. Ready to stand until the last, and perhaps we could even win. We had to believe.

"Ben, you're awake!" Max panted, and he gave me another slimy lick on the face for good measure. "You came to help us deal with the wargs."

"They're not wargs, they're warlocks," I said.

"Whatever, same thing ..."

"They're nothing like each other. Wargs look like very ugly versions of you, and warlocks look like very ugly versions of Asinda."

"Ben, concentrate! We need to fight!"

For sure we did, for the five warlocks assisting Lasinta had their staffs drawn, and they were closing in on us.

"We can handle them," Esme said. "But white magic only ... I don't want to see anyone using dark."

She shot me a look as if she knew all about my conversations with *Cana Dei*. But she looked at Seramina even longer, as if she posed a greater threat.

"Why is that Abyssinian always in charge?" Asinda asked.

Seramina shrugged. "Because she's a 'daughter of Bastet'."

"And I'm now a full-fledged member of the White Guard."

"Not a daughter of a goddess, though."

I decided not to point out that both Seramina and Asinda were in fact related to warlocks. I don't think that would have gone down too well.

"Submit," Lasinta bawled out again. "Submit or die!"

Whiskers, would this ever end?

Meanwhile, the warlocks fanned out in a semicircle in front of the Great Crystal. Their eyes had fire burning at the back of them. Clearly, they meant business.

"Draw staffs," Esme called.

Seramina and Asinda lifted theirs off their backs, and the crystals started glowing white immediately. Esme and I also summoned our staff bearers, and they lurched down to plunge our staffs in between our jaws. This time I didn't embrace the dark, but instead felt the cooling, soothing flow of white magic, easing my muscles. Making everything feel pure.

"Me too!" Max barked.

To my astonishment, he also summoned up a staff bearer. Except two hands appeared instead of one, and they were both clutching a tall mahogany staff, around a broad handle of woven hemp rope.

I blinked at it in disbelief. He hadn't told me about this ability. This wasn't fair. Max had two hands for a staff bearer, and they were armoured. Why couldn't I have that?

"Concentrate," Esme said. It always amazed me how she was able to talk normally with her staff in her mouth.

The warlocks shot beams out of their staffs, all of them purple and meeting at a central point above their heads. These became a purple cloud that deformed into the wispy shapes of two purple serpent mist-dragons. The summoned magical creatures charged forwards, spiralling towards us.

Seramina, Asinda, Esme and I also shot beams up into the sky, converging at a point. We formed a white ball that quickly transformed into a ball of grey feathers.

It took all our focus to ignite those feathers with brilliant flame, and from this a giant bird of fire – a phoenix – emerged resplendent. Its wings were even wider than Salanraja's, and it spread them out into the sky, sparks dripping off them. Then it flew towards the wisp-dragons.

The three magical creatures clashed in a brilliant display of purple and red. One wisp dragon tried to curl itself around the phoenix, strangling the fire out of it with its plumes of dark magic smoke.

Meanwhile, the phoenix kept flapping its wings, fanning the flames on its body, and keeping itself big enough that the wisp-dragon couldn't get a hold. At the same time it clawed with its great burning talons. With enough effort, it might be able to shred the dragons into faint plumes.

It took all of our collective concentration to keep the fires in the phoenix burning. But there were two dragons and only one phoenix. I could feel the energy leaching out of the phoenix's feathers. Soon they would wilt, and the phoenix would die.

"My turn!" Max whined in the dog language, unable to speak any other way with the staff in his mouth. "My crystal has given me a mission."

He turned his staff towards the crystal and out from it shot a beam of pure energy. I could feel it searing the air around it. Whiskers, it was so hot I thought we'd all be burned to a crisp.

The beam hit the Great Crystal right in the centre. The cracks within its structure glowed bright white.

"What are you doing, Max?" I whined in the dog language. "Stop! You'll break it!"

"We have no choice. My crystal told me to do this, Ben."

Even if I'd wanted to try and stop him, I didn't have a chance. His spell was just too powerful. Where had he got this from all of a sudden, anyway? It was dog ex machina ...

But then I'd known Max had to get his staff eventually. Yet another white magic user ... what had the crystals been thinking?

The Great Crystal splintered into a thousand different pieces, sending out mighty cracking sounds and quakes along the ground. Waves tossed up out of the swamp, and the island rocked as though it were a ship on a stormy sea. When the splinters hit the ground, they shivered into pieces again amid flashes of sparks, and again, and again, until they were only grains of sand, perhaps even fairy dust.

A shockwave followed from where the crystal had been, so powerful that it winked the phoenix and the mist dragons out of existence. It hit us then, sending us reeling. Both Esme and I dropped our staffs, and our staff bearers swooped in to recover them. Max, however, kept his staff firmly clasped in his jaws.

The beam from Lasinta shut off, and I thought she'd land on the ground with a thump. But instead there came a flurry of feathers, and a whiff of bird sweat.

Where Lasinta had been, a condor emerged and flew away. I turned my head to see five more birds lift off from where the warlocks had been. A hawk, a bald eagle, a vulture, a seagull, and a buzzard. They quickly gathered in formation and followed the condor towards the silver moon.

A swift retreat, and who knew where they would go next. But we also had no means of flying after them.

For now, it didn't matter – we had won. But we had also destroyed the Great Crystal in the process ...

Which meant our lives were about to change, and I feared this change would be for the worst.

✴ 42 ✴

SILVER LINING

The moon cast a silver lining on the curtain of retreating clouds. Soon these dispersed into much smaller clouds, and the moonlight glinting off them made them seem as if they were glowing. As the last vestiges of purple gas and rotten dark magic subsided, a canopy of stars wheeled out through the sky, and their reflections twinkled on the water.

A cool breeze washed out over the swampland, and some herons even dared to fly down for fish. Insects hummed and chirped amidst the reeds, and the whole landscape became a picture of placidity.

A landscape artist could have painted the most beautiful vista that night, whilst the dragons still slept and the fairy dust and sediment deposited by the wilted crystal shimmered in the moonlight, as if some of the stars had fallen from the sky.

Ripples poked up from the water – insects landing on the surface that would surely draw fish.

I sat watching the marshes for a moment, wondering what might happen next. Salanraja hadn't woken up yet, but my connection to her had returned. At the back of my mind, I could hear her murmuring in her dreams.

⤙ 235 ⤚

Still, something was missing that I'd grown to rely on since I'd moved to the First Dimension – all this time I'd had my crystal watching over me. Whenever I'd encountered danger, I had felt it pulsing at the back of my mind, the magic waiting. It had given me my magical gifts, and had guided me through my darkest moments. Now it was no longer there. The magic it had gifted to me was still with me, admittedly, but my connection to the crystal was not.

The breaking of the Great Crystal had broken that bond, and so I knew it would no longer be there to guide me through the darkness, to keep me safe from the threat of *Cana Dei*. I could even envision it my mind in Salanraja's chamber, devoid of light, not pulsing at all. If crystals could die, this was how it happened. They were cut off from their source.

In short, it felt as though I had lost a good friend.

I guess I should have counted myself lucky that our own crystals hadn't broken too. Such a thing would have killed us. It seemed that I still had everything that my crystal had given me; I knew I could still speak all languages and transform into a chimera and summon my staff bearer.

But I no longer had that connection to my crystal. It could help me no further.

Eventually, after several moments of grieving, I had an idea. I had not only lost my connection to my crystal, but my stomach was also complaining. Whiskers, I hadn't eaten since breakfast, with the exception of a few scraps of sugared beef.

"Esme," I asked. "Do you think we could catch a few fish?"

"Perhaps," Esme said, examining her claws. "I guess I'm just as peckish as you are."

"Don't you dare," Asinda said as she shouldered her staff.

"What?" I asked. "What's wrong with fish?"

"We've had enough problems with the fairies. You don't

learn this at Dragonsbond Academy, because you're not meant to go wandering off into the Faerie Realm, but we must never hunt here. Killing animals is strictly forbidden."

"But you fed us that beef," I said.

"Yes, but I got it from the Fourth Dimension. Even that might have been frowned upon if any fairies had seen me."

"The Oracle Fairy must have seen it."

"The Oracle Fairy isn't a fairy, but a tree," Asinda said.

"Sugared beef strands," Max barked, understanding completely. "I want sugared beef strands."

He refused to speak in the human language, and so in his language he didn't have a proper way of describing it.

"If he's asking for 'beef joiky', we've eaten it all."

"You've got to be joking," Esme said.

Asinda shook her head.

"So we can't eat meat here," I said, "and we're stuck in the fairy realm."

"Hopefully they'll get us out soon ..."

"Look," Seramina said. "They're waking up now."

Indeed, golden wisps began to rise from the ground, adding even more lustre to the scene. They didn't take long to find their wings, and soon they were darting around like fireflies. For a moment I wondered if I had died and gone to cat heaven. But then I realised that in cat heaven there would be plenty more food.

My tummy growled loudly at me, as a golden plume of smoke formed above the island. The king of Faerini, King So'ta, appeared before us. His red silk robe trailed in the water, and I wondered if it could get wet in his glamoured form.

"Will one of you care to explain what happened here?" He looked around at the purple crystals strewn across the ground – the dead shells of the manipulators that we had battled before. His eyebrows furrowed. "Burns and dragonfire – I hope that you're not responsible for this."

We all exchanged glances, wondering who could best explain the situation. Indeed, if King So'ta remembered nothing then we would have a hard time convincing him.

Esme and Asinda both stepped forward at the same time. But they didn't have a chance to say a word before another golden plume developed and Queen Ca'mun stepped into the fray.

"King So'ta," she said in her high-pitched voice, and she offered him her hand. "It's a pleasure to once again make your acquaintance."

King So'ta leaned down and kissed the back of the fairy queen's hand. "The pleasure is all mine. Now, do you have an explanation for whatever chaos has occurred here, please? Because it seems the Aisean Wetlands are in complete disarray."

We allowed Queen Ca'mun to explain everything. So'ta at first found it hard to accept that the warlocks had hypnotised the whole of Faerini. But as to that, Ca'mun pointed out that Astravar had once managed to turn a large subset of their population into Cat Sidhe, and also the king's son Ta'lon had found himself hypnotised into doing Lasinta's bidding numerous times. Regarding the latter, So'ta expressed his deepest apologies. Of course, Ta'lon never revealed himself to express this in person.

As Ca'mun and So'ta talked, Esme and I turned our attention to grooming any remaining traces of dark magic out of our fur. Our routine was meticulous, and we made sure not to miss a speck. After we'd been doing it for a while, Max sat beside us and also groomed himself in that strange and inefficient way that dogs have, involving much more paws than tongue.

After some time spent listening to Ca'mun's long and

drawn-out story, and when I was thoroughly clean, Salanraja woke up. I felt clarity return to my mind, and I turned to see her bright yellow eye gleaming only several yards away from me. But I wasn't looking at just one eye; I saw hundreds of other dragons opening their eyes at the same time. Whatever dark hold the converted Great Crystal had had on them must have finally dissipated into the soil. Not one trace of rotten vegetable juice remained in the air.

The dragons grunted and groaned, and I even heard a couple of roars. Most of them were probably wondering how the whiskers they had ended up lying on this island surrounded by swamps.

"*Bengie,*" Salanraja said. "*Is that you? Gracious demons, I survived.*"

"*Salanraja,*" I said. "*I saw you within the darkness, and I really thought you were going to choose death. I'm so glad you made it through.*"

I really meant it, too. Though my dragon could be annoying sometimes, I didn't know what I would do without her. My bond with her had taken me on a journey from a regular housecat to the mighty Dragoncat I was today. Somehow, I knew I still had far to go.

"*I'm glad too,*" Salanraja said. "*But I wasn't in control of my mind in that place. I don't know what I would have chosen ... I fear I might have been about to let myself submit.*"

I remembered *Cana Dei* looming over me then, how tempted I had been to turn to its cause. It would have been so easy just to embrace the darkness. And now that the crystal had gone and only uncertainty lay ahead, I had a feeling that the temptation would only get stronger.

"*We lost our crystal, Salanraja,*" I said. "*Max got his staff, and he used it to destroy the Great Crystal. The bond no longer exists.*"

I felt Salanraja take a deep breath. "*I know. I heard many times from Olan that the Great Crystal foretold this prophecy. It had seen its own demise. But it has a twin somewhere, deep within the Crystal Mountains. If we can recover that, then we can perhaps repair the bond."*

"And what do we do until then?" I asked.

After the dragons had woken up, and many of them had taken off to scout the surrounding terrain, my human companions woke too. Rine and Ange ran to hold each other in their arms. Kamino also embraced Bellari, but all the time she kept looking over at the other couple. I narrowed my eyes.

I knew it – Bellari wasn't over Rine, and was probably working out ways to get back together with him even as the muscular Kamino attempted to cuddle her. Well, I was here to make sure she wouldn't cause any problems. I didn't care if she was 'High Prefect' or not, I wasn't going to let some allergic teenager ruin my plans for a comfortable retirement.

Aleam picked himself up with the aid of his staff. He glanced at the four teenagers, probably decided to leave them to their nuzzling, and instead hobbled over to talk to us.

"So how are my three animals doing?" he asked.

Max was the first to answer. "I'm good!" he barked. "Nice to see you, old man! You are kind, old man!"

Aleam looked down at him, his eyes wide. "It's as if he can understand me," he said.

"He can now," I said in the human language.

"So you'd better be careful what you say," Esme said.

Aleam smiled. "I wondered when he'd get his abilities."

"Oh, he's got the full range of them," I said. "Including his staff, a two-handed staff bearer with gauntlets, and some more powerful magic than I'd have ever imagined."

I took a deep breath. I wasn't sure how to break the news to Aleam; I also wasn't sure how much he'd worked out for himself. He must also feel that slight space in his heart where his bond with his crystal had been, but that didn't mean he knew why it was there.

"What is it, Ben?" Aleam asked.

"We've lost the Great Crystal," I said. "Max's magic destroyed it, and his crystal told him to do it, but I don't know what any of us are going to do next. There's so much uncertainty, Aleam. How can we survive without our crystals?"

I guess a twisted part of me wanted to agitate Aleam as well, to drag him with me into a spiral of anxiety. Instead, he calmly lowered his head. He looked back at his great white dragon, Olan, who stood with her tall neck craned, staring out over the waters as if she also quite fancied some fish.

Esme, my *companion,* sidled up next to me and lay down by my side, as if to provide a little comfort. But this time she left the job of providing words of wisdom to Aleam.

"You know, Ben," he said, "have I ever told you how I used to chase sunsets?"

"No," I said. "Why would you ever do that?"

"Well, when I was young, I used to go on hikes with my friends in the foothills of the Crystal Mountains. We would climb the peaks, but we always had to reach the top before sunset, sometimes even running to make it to the summit."

I growled slightly. "Hiking," I said. "Such a pointless activity."

Aleam chuckled. "I guess that's what I learned; there was no point in racing to get to the top of the peak. You could just as well watch the sunset from the valley, and it's just as beautiful. In fact it adds an air of mystery to it – not quite knowing how the other side of the hill is lit, and being comfortable with not being able to see the other side at the end of the day. It makes the journey much more pleasant, don't you think?"

I lowered myself down onto my paws and stretched them, as I remembered a word from a distant language. "The feeling of that which remains unseen. The Japanese have a word for it, I believe."

Aleam raised one eyebrow. "The Japanese?"

"They're a civilisation in my world. Lots of famous and masterful swordsmen throughout history. I hear they also have a lot of respect for cats."

"And what was the word?" Aleam asked.

"*Yugen*," I said. "They call it *yugen*."

Aleam paused, as if rolling the word around in his mind. "I like that," he said. "I think I'll use that from now on. *Yugen* ..."

He smiled, and we turned our heads to look out over the water. Together, our gazes drifted off into the distance beyond that which remained unseen.

AN OLD AND FAITHFUL
COMPANION

We milled around the Aisean Wetlands, before Ca'mun and So'ta offered to use their magic to teleport all the dragon riders and every dragon present back to Dragonsbond Academy. After everything that had transpired, they also gave us permission to sleep in the Faerie Realm for the night, so long as no one left the castle.

Then, at the break of dawn – when fairy magic was apparently the strongest – the fairies would work their spells on the school to send it back to the First Dimension.

King So'ta as a form of apology offered to pay any tributes that Ca'mun had said she was going to collect from King Garmin.

But I didn't want to travel back to the academy, for I knew that I still had to look out for my former *companion*. Salanraja said that she'd reached out to the Cat Sidhe's dragon, Kada, and that they were out there feeling terribly lost. I needed to go and help her; I cared about her after all.

At first Ca'mun didn't want to let me, but So'ta butted in, saying he thought it was a good idea. The way that he said it, it made me realise that things weren't good for Ta'ra. The fact that Ta'lon had not revealed himself supported my belief.

"Is Ta'lon …" I asked King So'ta, who was standing tall before me. "Is he dead?"

"Burns and dragonfire, no," So'ta replied. "He's quite well … it's just, well, you should speak to Ta'ra."

I didn't waste another minute. I flew south on Salanraja's back, nestled safely inside her corridor of spikes as I searched the rolling scene below. The moon had now wheeled high in the sky, and the light from it sent pretty patterns over the ripples in the marshes. Salanraja flew low and very carefully, so that I could search for the cat and dragon. The loss of the Great Crystal had apparently damaged some abilities that dragons took for granted, including the ability to pinpoint exactly where Kada was.

We found them on the top of a limestone promontory, where the wetlands flowed out of a rocky karst. Mist fringed the landscape's basin, and above it both the cat and the dragon were taking turns yowling at the moon.

Ta'ra would have been invisible if it weren't for the moon shining off the white diamond patch on her chest. The rest of her black fur blended in with darkness. But then, the dwarf dragon Kada was much easier to see, his chalk-white scales seeming to dance in the moonlight.

I'm not sure if they even saw us approach, but then, it was dark. Salanraja had definitely announced to Kada that we were coming, but I guess she hadn't announced when we would arrive. But they did not seem to care.

Salanraja landed gracefully on a patch of moss, and lowered her body to allow me to clamber off. I stalked up to Ta'ra, who turned her head to face me.

"Go away, Ben," she said. "I want to be left alone."

"Really?" I asked. "Is that how you greet your old *companion*."

"Old *companion* ..." She raised her head to look at the moon. "I've ruined everything, Ben. Ta'lon just visited me here, and he said he doesn't want this anymore; his *kingdom* doesn't want it. When he made those promises, he was being influenced by Lasinta. I'm nothing to him – I'm not welcome inside his court. I mean, did you feel it? Something has broken inside of me."

"It broke inside all of us," I said. "We had to break the Great Crystal to stop Lasinta from destroying the worlds."

We both fell silent. I'm not sure how much she knew about the implications of this; I'm not sure how much any of us knew about them, to be honest.

A bat flitted by overhead. I watched it, wondering if I could catch it. Ta'ra once again yowled, and Kada howled like a wolf. The Cat Sidhe smelled more of moss now than of lavender, and she had patches of the stuff on her fur.

"Come back with us," I said to Ta'ra.

She twitched up her ears and her eyes glinted for a moment. "What?"

"You still have a life in Dragonsbond Academy, and you have people who love you there. Rine ... Ange ... Seramina ... Aleam ... me."

Ta'ra blinked on the final word in that sentence. Not a slow blink, but one of disbelief. "You don't love me, Ben. You were born a cat ... no one ever taught you what love is."

"That's not true," I said. "I care about you a lot, Ta'ra. And you already know that I dream about you. I also think about you – I think about you a lot."

"But you have Esme now ... a new *companion*. A daughter of Bastet."

"I do have Esme," I said. I remembered Rine's dream, and thought it couldn't do any harm trying. "But tomcats can have two companions."

She narrowed her bright green eyes. Suddenly I sensed a

spike of anger in the air, but at least I'd got her to feel something. "You've got to be kidding," she said. "Two companions? Who do you think you are, Ben?"

"I am Dra—" I stopped myself just in time. Common sense told me that the descendant of the great Asian leopard cat line probably wasn't going to work here. "Let's just take things one step at a time, shall we?"

"Fine," Ta'ra said, and she glanced over at Kada. "You're right, I should return to Dragonsbond Academy. But don't think for a moment I'll be your second *companion*. I'm a princess, Ben ... a princess."

I felt for a moment that I should add something. But there was nothing more to say. Instead, I watched Ta'ra stalk towards her dwarf dragon and I also climbed up Salanraja's tail.

"*Way to go, Bengie,*" she said once I was safely in her corridor of spikes. "*I knew you could you do it.*"

"*Just shut up right there,*" I said. "*Let's just fly and not talk about this subject ever again.*"

"*As you wish,*" she replied with a hint of mischief in her voice.

Thus, Kada and Salanraja carried us both under the high full moon, which bathed our fur in a strange, mystical warmth. Together we flew blissfully into *yugen*, blissfully into the unknown.

ACKNOWLEDGMENTS

THANK YOU TO Tarryn Thomas for editing and proofreading this book – your continuing feedback is invaluable, and I promise not to capitalise any more spaniels. Many thanks also to my family, particularly my parents for their continuing support and my dear wife Ola for reading the early drafts of the novel and providing valuable input.

Also, thank you as always to my ARC team. I really appreciate all the work that you put in helping to promote my novels.

Finally, thank you to every single reader – I appreciate everything that you do to support authors and the world of literature at large.

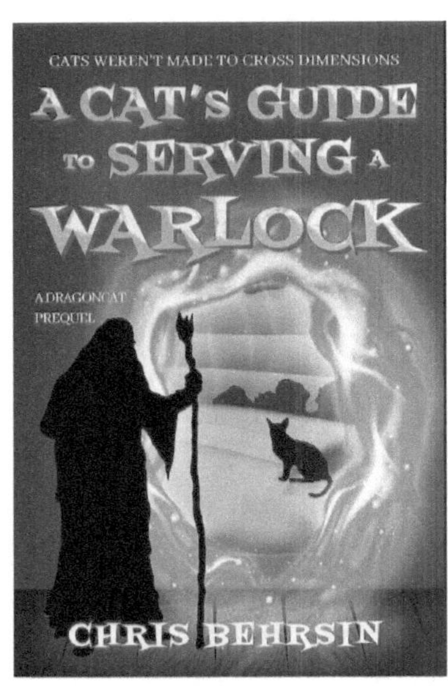

THANK YOU FOR READING "*A Cat's Guide to Dreaming of Fairies*". I hope that you enjoyed it and that it added value for you in your every day life.

I have written a prequel novelette to this series entitled "*A Cat's Guide to Serving a Warlock*", which you can download for free by signing up to my newsletter at https://chris-behrsin.com/servingawarlock.

I send bi-monthly emails with promos, giveaways, information about new releases and news about what's going on in my life in general.

www.ingramcontent.com/pod-product-compliance
Lightning Source LLC
Chambersburg PA
CBHW031421200726
48285CB00018BA/2606